THE LATIN LOVER

THE
LATIN
LOVER
P.M.

Nexus

First published in Great Britain in 1991 by
Nexus
338 Ladbroke Grove
London W10 5AH

Translated from the French *Memoires d'un adolescent
clandestin*
copyright © Mercure de France 1989
Translated by Sue Dyson
Translation copyright © Nexus Books 1991

Phototypeset by Intype, London
Printed in Great Britain by
Cox & Wyman Ltd, Reading, Berks

ISBN 0 352 328029

'I discovered her photo, yellowed with age, in an old shoe-box belonging to my father. It was an old snapshot dating from the Forties. My mother looked scarcely more than an adolescent. Her smile radiated joie de vivre. She was wearing a lace blouse fastened at the neck with a row of buttons running down between her curving breasts, and she stood arms folded and leaning against a table. Her eyes were bright. I wasn't yet sure of their colour, for my father never mentioned it. I pressed the fifteen-year-old photo to my heart, then to my lips. Then I put it into my pocket and ran out into the streets of the town. The memory of her glowed in my mind. I was obsessed with it. My heart was filled with a mixture of happiness and anguish. I ran towards the port as if I were going to meet her, for I had never really seen my mother. Except perhaps one night: just one single night.

I was awakened by a body pressing itself against me, covering me with kisses; then suddenly there was a harsh light, noise, weeping – and then nothing more.'

1

That was how Reinaldo began his story – clear-headed and in that melancholy voice of his. He had no problem remembering now, his mauve-grey eyes gazing into mine. That night, he even went so far as to tell me that while he was still in the womb he had felt bad vibrations. And as he told his story he would break into ironic laughter.

We were in a little cabaret club called Au Dix, in rue Odéon, where many foreigners used to go. A soft, red light shone on our faces through the clouds of cigarette-smoke. A juke-box – something of an anachronism – played hit-songs old and new, chosen by the customers.

Reinaldo was a South American: either Venezuelan or Colombian, I wasn't sure yet. He spoke excellent French, peppered with Spanish. You couldn't gauge his age from his copper skin or his collar-length black hair, broad shoulders, or his hands which moved expressively when he spoke. Perhaps he was in his forties or fifties? A handsome man.

2

I was sitting on a bar-stool facing the counter and drinking a martini and gin when the bartender asked me how things were going. I replied: 'Oh! What a life!' It was then that Reinaldo addressed me.

'What a life? What terrible experiences can you possibly have had? You seem very young still, scarcely halfway through your life, and yet it's a burden already? Look at all these marvellous women all around you, listen to all that laughter, look at those faces, worries shed after a few drinks, and look at yourself: there's nothing on your face or in your eyes which expresses some curse within you! . . .'

He was looking me straight in the eye, and I marvelled at his tirade. I bought him another drink and had one myself. I had to give him an answer – the barman had given me the wink, to make sure that I realized I was talking to a real character – and so I began a conversation with him.

'No! But I did know a strange woman who disappeared from my life overnight. That's why I said that.'

'She would not be a strange woman if she hadn't left her share of dark secrets behind her. That's what adds spice to life. If I told you the story of my life, there would be a host of things which you could never make sense of!'

The corners of his mouth curled upwards in the beginnings of a smile. I listened to him. He motioned to the barman, and our glasses were refilled.

'There you are, Monsieur Reinaldo,' said the bartender.

It was then that I noticed that he was addressed only by his first name, preceded by a very deferential *Monsieur*. Reinaldo was wearing a beige suit of English cut, a shirt with narrow strips and a lotus-patterned tie. The juke-box was playing Sinatra's 'Strangers in the Night'. And the room was slowly filling up. The air-conditioner blew out cool draughts. It was the beginning of summer. Paris was becoming sensual.

Bodies envigorated by the new season, launched themselves energetically on the trail; tongues were loosened. Reinaldo made clear what he meant by the expression: a terrible life!

I asked him where he came from. Who was he? Why had he talked of curses and elusive women? His only response was a faint smile.

'When I went to the port, I did not know if I could get aboard a steamer bound for Spain. I had two possibilities left: either go to Barranquilla, the other big port, or stay where I was at La Guaira. My meagre savings weren't enough to take a bus to the Colombia/Venezuela frontier. And so I walked along the quays. I listened to the announcements. I spent more than three hours like this, going from one point to another. At last I heard a voice announcing a departure for Spain. I dashed to the quay where the steamer was docked. I can still remember its name: *La Estrellitta*.

Men, who seemed to be visitors, were about to follow a guide who was signalling with his arms and describing the boat to them. Silently I moved closer, and listened intently. They took no notice of me. They walked up the gangplank and I waited until they were on the deck before I followed them. I looked behind me: there was no one on the quayside. In an instant I was on deck, and I moved off in the opposite direction to their tour. I stole down a companion-way, then another, and found myself in a little corridor which undoubtedly contained the crew's cabins. There were names on the doors. I had a good look round, listening in case someone was coming. Then I continued on my way until I came to the galleys. At the end of this narrowing corridor I noticed a variety of doors and big wooden cupboards. I opened one, which contained linen; then another, which had crockery piled up inside. Obviously I was in the storeroom. Suddenly, as I opened another cupboard, I heard someone coming down the stairs. I hid in the cupboard and held my breath. I didn't move, for fear that I would be discovered. Footsteps came closer and the boat's siren boomed out. Was this the first signal for embarkation, or maybe even sailing? I had lost all sense of time. My ears were buzzing. The noise of people rushing about grew louder. Doors were opened and slammed with loud shouts. I crouched down in my hiding-place and kept my ears open for the slightest sound. I heard a second siren.

The siren gave three very long whistles. The ship was preparing to cast off. Then I sensed that we were moving away from the quayside. The siren sounded three more times. My heart was pounding. I knew that I would never come back again to Venezuela. As I left the port of La Guaira, I felt I had won my freedom. But in the meantime I was imprisoned in a broom cupboard . . .'

Reinaldo caught his breath and emptied the dregs of his glass. In spite of all the noise and chatter we two had set foot on another planet. I listened to him and wondered why he had talked so much to me about women. I gave a questioning pout. He understood immediately: I wanted to know what happened next.

The barman served us again. Reinaldo continued his tale with the same intensity of recall.

'At that time I was about sixteen. But I looked older. Which made a lot of things easier for me. Especially when it came to women. It all began on that voyage. There I was, shut away in my hiding-place in all that heat for a good three hours. No one had come to disturb me. So I decided to get out of the cupboard. The noises and voices had faded away. The crewmen were no doubt busy with their respective tasks. Once I had carefully extracted myself from the cupboard, I climbed the stairs I had used before. I was covered in sweat, my skin clammy and a rancid odour of dust all over my body. Climbing the second staircase took me to the deck. I didn't see a single member of the crew. Men and women – with towels in their hands – were walking towards another part of the boat, the highest level, where there was no doubt a swimming-pool. I realized that, the way I was dressed, I must look pretty weird. So I took off my short-sleeved shirt and followed these bathers. I was close to the changing-rooms. I used the shower. And dived immediately into the water. At last, I felt confident! When I came to the surface, I swam a few lengths and leant against the side of the pool. Then suddenly I heard a shout behind me and a girl dived in just over my head.

To tell the truth, she'd been pushed. I drew myself up a little and saw a very beautiful girl with long, jet-black hair. I caught her eye and she laughed, putting her hand over her mouth. Her victim was swimming with difficulty and trying to get a grip on the edge of the pool. I held my hand out to her and pulled her towards me. When she had managed to get her breath back, she thanked me.

'I didn't hurt you when I fell in, did I?' she said. 'Please excuse us, my sister loves playing that game.'

'Oh, don't worry,' I replied. 'Do you want to come out?'

'Yes please.'

I slid out of the pool and grabbed hold of her hands. Her sister was standing behind us. They began to laugh. I laughed too, to be part of the game. They were both as brown as each other and looked to be about nineteen and twenty. It was Carlotta, the elder girl, who had pushed her sister Yolanda into the water. Yolanda had curly hair, long English-style ringlets, dark, almond-shaped eyes and an agreeably curvaceous body. Her sister, Carlotta, was more slender. Very personable she was, and already with all the look of a young woman very sure of herself. Yolanda seemed shyer, reserved, but her smile was roguish. They invited me to the bar for a glass of fruit juice. Once more I felt safe.

They both put on bathrobes while I followed them in my swimming-trunks – the only ones I had. Yolanda was casting coy glances at me whilst Carlotta was still joking about the surprise-effect of the dive.

I learned that they were travelling with their aunt. An adorable young woman who never got on their nerves. The girls could do whatever they wanted. When they asked me a few questions about my trip, I remained wary; I wondered if I would have to tell them everything. When we had drunk our fruit juice, we went for a bathe. Yolanda asked me some more questions. She wanted to know if I was going to make a stopover in the Canary Isles, at Santa Cruz de Tenerife. It was one bit of information she'd given me about the journey. I told her that I was going to Spain, but that I did not know how long I would stay there. She could see quite clearly that I did not want to talk about my journey. She took my hand and led me to the other side of the deck. Meanwhile, Carlotta was swimming in the pool. I felt a little surprised. But already a certain complicity was springing up between us. She talked to me about her sister, with whom she shared everything. I listened to her, staring into her eyes. I wanted to kiss her because I felt good with her. I approached her and gave her a kiss on the cheek, which she returned immediately. For a short time we were silent. I gave a sidelong glance at the pool and saw Carlotta getting out. She smiled at me as well as at her sister. We waved to her and Yolanda called to her. Then I began asking her:

'Yolanda, what do you do?'

'I'm a student at a school of dance and music – so is my sister, but she wants to be an actress, to go to drama school. But I'd like to sing later on. I don't know if we'll stay in La Guaira next year. Our parents want to move to Caracas, or they may send us to Rio de Janeiro. Down there, both of us could think about our studies and our careers. Also, we will be spending part of our holidays with our dear aunt. She's a pianist and a music teacher.'

Carlotta joined us. The two sisters winked at each other. She leaned over my shoulder, gave me a delicate kiss on the cheek and thanked me for taking care of Yolanda. They had superb bodies and a rare lightness of movement.

As she sat down next to us, Carlotta brushed my leg. The tips of her breasts were visible through the fabric of her swimming-costume, which formed a triangle over her fine breasts whose nipples seemed to me to be extremely pointed. She was constantly running her tongue over her lips, as though she were executing some secret sign language. I still did not react and my eyes travelled from one to the other. Yolanda held herself very upright, so that her round breasts were thrusting forward. I was disconcerted by such sensual presences.

It was the end of the afternoon. I had no watch and at that moment time meant nothing to me. Was I going to spend the night in the broom-cupboard? My two new compa..ions made me feel secure and I told myself: what the hell!

Yolanda and Carlotta invited me to follow them into their cabin. They wanted to get changed and take a shower before dressing for dinner and joining their aunt. So I picked up my clothes, which were piled up in a corner, and followed them. Carlotta asked me if I wanted to tell my parents where I was. I said no. Yolanda seemed surprised. Then they took me by the hand and we went into their cabin.

They shared the same cabin. Their aunt was in another, larger one, next to theirs. I didn't know how to explain to them that I was a stowaway. I decided to let nature take its course.

When we entered the cabin, Carlotta and Yolanda took off their bathrobes. At that moment, and with the utmost innocence, Carlotta asked me my age. I replied: sixteen. She told me that she was five years older and that Yolanda was twenty. They were proud of being older than I was. But they said that they would have taken me for eighteen, at least. They flirted and Carlotta took off her swimming-costume in front of me: Yolanda followed suit. I turned away to show that I was embarrassed. I was deeply affected and turned back towards them when they called me. Their breasts were free and moved in time to their laughter. They ogled me, assuring me that I was not embarrassing them in the least. Carlotta drew me towards her and asked me to look at her breasts and

11

those of Yolanda. She wanted me to give her my impressions of them.

'You can look, Reinaldo,' she said. 'We are artistes, you know!'

I said 'yes', inaudibly, and nodded my head. I was in the most frightful state of excitement. Yolanda stood beside her sister and offered me her breasts which were shaped like two oval water-melons. I loved the purity of their contours. Carlotta's, which were less full, were more like two juicy mangoes, ending in black grapes at the tips. They looked at themselves in a mirror, standing on tiptoe. I saw the purity of their hips, and their flowing curve down towards the thighs. They turned back towards me again and laughed gleefully. I followed suit, so as to show my solidarity. Then Carlotta took hold of my hand and placed it on her breasts.

'You can touch them, they're hard!' she said, pressing my hand against her breast.

I checked out Carlotta's breasts, and she invited me to feel Yolanda's – she was getting impatient. As I hesitated, she ordered me to take hold of them with both hands. And so I massaged their breasts in a sort of strange manual ritual. Meanwhile, my blood was starting to boil with excitement. The girls asked me to compare them. So, in each hand, I held a different breast. I caressed them, cupping each, assessing their size and volume. Carlotta seemed excited, for she was rocking from one foot to the other, whilst Yolanda seemed transfixed in the sensual pleasure which my somewhat awkward caresses were giving her.

Carlotta put an end to this exercise. She walked towards the shower, leaving me alone with Yolanda, who had begun to lay out her clothes.

Suddenly, she turned towards me and drew me towards the bunk. I wasn't very enterprising in those days. She put her hand round my hips and gave me a burning kiss. I felt my heart thumping against her quivering bosom. I was thoroughly disconcerted; I was thinking of the aunt who might turn up at any moment, and I was thinking about my journey and the hiding-place where I would have to go at nightfall. Yolanda's movements were a little awkward but her style aroused me. I pressed my lips against hers, then kissed the nape of her neck. She took my hand and moved it towards her breasts, whispering in my ear: 'You really like them, don't you?' What could I say? They were keeping me aroused, whilst her body soothed me. 'They're beautiful,' I replied. At that moment, Yolanda moved slightly away from me and showed them to me again. I paid her another compliment, which comforted her. She stood up and left me on the bunk. She took a bath-towel and laid it on an armchair. Then she gave me a look whose significance was lost on me.

Yolanda called to her sister, who was running the shower. Carlotta asked her to come in. Yolanda asked me if I wanted to have a shower here or in my cabin. I remained nonplussed. I didn't give a comprehensible reply. She came towards me and pouted like a winsome she-cat. I did not know how to avoid this burning look. Yolanda unfastened my belt and pulled down my trousers. I was completely under her spell and abandoned myself to her. I was still wearing my swimming-trunks and remained wild-eyed, in that cabin, under the gaze of Yolanda who went to join her sister in the shower. But before she did so, she took off her panties and threw them into the room.

I heard them laughing and splashing about under the shower. From time to time, Yolanda cried out and Carlotta was laughing at the top of her voice. It was Carlotta who, after a few minutes, invited me to join them. I thanked them but said I could wait. They gave an 'oh!' of astonishment, followed by even louder laughter. 'I'm coming to get you!' said Carlotta. What was I to think? Really, I looked just like a little boy. And Carlotta came out of the shower, soaking wet, and ran towards me. She dragged me towards the shower – with little resistance on my part as I looked at her completely naked body and detected her dark pubis. I was overcome by the oddest sensation. My penis twisted about and grew longer inside my swimming-trunks, which when I entered the tiny shower-area, Carlotta and Yolanda tore off. Yolanda was rubbing herself with a soapy washing-mitt. I was standing between them. And Carlotta asked me to rub her back. Which I did, without saying a word. Yolanda, who was behind me, rinsed me down. I felt her firm breasts on my back and her thighs on my buttocks.

She rubbed a bar of soap over my back and hips, then down towards my legs. Carlotta turned round and she too pressed her breasts against my chest. She guided my hand towards her breasts and I rubbed her bust, her belly and thighs. She put her hands on my hips and the contact of her skin made me shiver. The hot water was flowing over our naked bodies. My prick was erect and I was ashamed of it. There was no way they could not have noticed it.

I followed the movement of this torrid shower. Yolanda bent down and picked up the soap which had slipped out of her hand. She touched my prick with her arm. It was like an electric shock. I burst out laughing, which relaxed the atmosphere. They began to laugh too. Then Yolanda wanted to do the same for me. First of all, she began to rub my legs. Very slowly, she moved up my thighs. Carlotta told her to be careful when she reached my prick. Yolanda reassured her, telling her that she had gentle hands. Carlotta was standing behind me, pouring water on my back and pretending to wash my backside with soap. I had the impression that she was caressing it. Yolanda surprised me when quite suddenly, she placed her hand on my prick. She winked at me, then slid her hand around and through my thighs, then returned to my prick with the utmost gentleness. It grew hard between her fingers. Carlotta, who was already very excited, took my hand and drew it towards her pubis. My fingers moved around it, whilst she leant towards my neck and planted a kiss upon it, with a wet, sucking noise. It was as though I were the prisoner of their embraces: lithe, throbbing embraces. Yolanda, who was taking the greatest care with me, was licking my back. Carlotta asked her to leave her alone for a moment, so that she could take care of me. Yolanda left the shower, indicating that she would come back later to dry me off.

Carlotta thought I was too timid. She gave me some advice, made me laugh again and again to relax me, and drew close to my lips which she seized greedily.

Her tongue worked its way into my mouth, she rubbed herself against me, one leg in between mine. I felt a warmth spreading through my lower belly and my prick was stretched so taut that it hurt. Carlotta revelled in this carnal yet innocent contact. Innocent, because my shyness was slowly communicating itself to her. I was so timid that I contained my arousal. She moved away from my crotch and slid her hand on to my burning prick. I moved away slightly, but with a few kisses she reassured me and took hold of my hand, guiding it on to her pubis. For a short while I rubbed her pubis, which felt soft. Then I slid my fingers into the folds of her dripping-wet vulva. She moved my hand and pushed it hard between the lips of her cunt. I pressed my prick against her thigh and masturbated her as she wanted me to. She gripped me close and gave a stifled cry into my neck. I had a huge hard-on but did not have an emission. This situation seemed unreal to me. Carlotta drew away and kissed me very tenderly on the mouth, then called to Yolanda to come and finish having a shower with me. She stayed with Yolanda to make me laugh a little. When Yolanda came into the shower, I hid my prick which was still erect. She moved up to me and stretched out her hand to uncover me and see my penis, then gave a hearty laugh, which relaxed me. The kissing started: first she kissed me on the cheeks and then on the mouth. I drew a long kiss from her, holding her to me, her breasts pressed tight against my torso. Her tongue wriggled about playfully inside my mouth. She was making me experience even greater and more varied sensations than her sister had done. Her hand moved down the length of my back and caressed my buttocks, then grabbed hold of my prick. I did the same, pushing my fingers into her cunt which trembled at each movement of my hand. She was quicker than I was. Immediately, she drew a great growl of pleasure from me. I ejaculated against her belly, and she saw the liquid shooting in spurts, for I had held myself back for too long. She was thrilled. And I continued to caress her until she was drunk with pleasure. And she caressed herself with my sperm, which she spread between her thighs.

We left the shower to join Carlotta. Once again, they gave each other a look of complicity. I got dressed very quickly. Yolanda did the same. They wore brightly coloured dresses: violet, red and yellow.

When at last they were ready, they asked me if I would like to join them later for dinner with their aunt. I was embarrassed. But at that moment I felt more at ease, although there might be a risk.

After walking up and down in their cabin, I made up my mind to tell them all my troubles. I looked them straight in the eye and warned them that what I was about to tell them was deadly serious. Deep down, I was thinking about their aunt. I wondered if it wasn't better to put back the hour of my confession for a day, in order to win over their complete trust. There was always the broom cupboard solution. But could I still hide there?

They listened to me in utter silence, expressing first astonishment then stupefaction. Now they understood why I was so mysterious and reserved. My courage greatly impressed them and they tried to find solutions, but no logical one sprang to mind.

First of all, their aunt had to be brought in on the secret. Carlotta and Yolanda persuaded me that she would be a true friend.

Time passed. It was almost time for dinner in the great dining-hall, and the aunt was due to call for them at their cabin at around seven-thirty. Yolanda couldn't wait any longer, impatiently opening the cabin door over and over again to see if she was coming. Carlotta calmed her down. And she decided that she would be the spokesman when the time came to reveal my adventure to her.

The aunt arrived a little after the time she had said. Yolanda and Carlotta greeted her affectionately.

When she saw me, she commented: 'So, you've already found yourselves a friend!' Then she apologized for her lateness. She had met a musician on the boat and had had a drink with him. At that moment, Carlotta very quickly took up the conversation and introduced me to her aunt, whose first name was Maria. Carlotta glanced at me reassuringly, but it wasn't enough. I just wanted to go off on my own and leave them. Carlotta understood that I was feeling uneasy. And Yolanda winked at me whilst her aunt looked at herself in the mirror and arranged her hair.

Carlotta began to talk to her aunt, who seemed to be a charming woman and very young. She must have been about thirty-five. She waved her hands about animatedly. She seemed to adore her little nieces. Then Carlotta told her my story. Here and there, Yolanda added a few details to her sister's account, to give my story emotional appeal.

After listening to Carlotta and Yolanda, aunt Maria surveyed the situation. She came up to me – amazingly – and took my hands. She ordered me to sit down, for I had remained standing, unsure of her reaction. The girls surrounded their aunt, warmly. She asked me my age. And a thousand other things. I answered truthfully.

Aunt Maria decided it would be better if I did not come and have dinner with them in the boat's main dining-saloon. The captain would ask if I was a member of the family. He might check with the list of passengers. Aunt Maria would take me into her cabin, as it had a second bunk. As for meals, she would bring me food secretly. Carlotta and Yolanda cried out for joy and hugged their aunt. Then she put her arms round my shoulders and reassured me with a mother's kiss. My heart had stopped its infernal pounding. But I was now wondering how I was going to reach the next port. For the moment, I would leave everything to them.

It was eight o'clock and they went to dinner. Aunt Maria asked me to stay in the cabin until they returned. Carlotta and Yolanda kissed me. Aunt Maria saw that her nieces had formed a firm friendship with me.

I accompanied them as far as the door, which I closed behind them, and heard Aunt Maria say to them: 'You really like that boy, don't you?' But I didn't hear Carlotta and Yolanda's replies.

Nevertheless, I imagined them: for I had the proof.

Now I could relax on the bunk, and enjoy the silence. There were no more sounds in my head. I took in deep lungfuls of air and had no further reason to worry. I thought about my fortnight's crossing in these conditions. What would each day bring on this steamer with Carlotta, Yolanda and Aunt Maria?

A whole host of incongruous images crowded into my brain. I could still see myself walking along the quayside at La Guaira, my hasty embarkation and all that you know, *dear comrade*. That cabin was like a safety-valve. Deep within myself, I thought tirelessly

about the goal of my journey. Would I succeed in
finding what I was looking for?'

'Whilst they were at dinner, the sense of melancholy which had spread through me turned into joy, a secret joy. I lay still on the bunk.

When Carlotta, Yolanda and Aunt Maria came back, I gave a start of surprise. They brought some fruit, cheese and vegetables. I was very hungry and ate it all with relish. Aunt Maria took stock of the situation once more. Would the journey pass without any risks? We'd have to prepare for the stopover at Santa Cruz de Tenerife before continuing on to Spain.

It was getting late. Aunt Maria kissed her nieces. I did the same and followed her into her cabin. There, she showed me my bunk. She gave me a shirt which would serve as my pyjamas. She took off her make-up in the bathroom, then undressed in front of me before putting on a black silk nightgown. I got undressed, but kept my trunks on. She questioned me about my luggage. I replied that I had put a small parcel in the broom cupboard. She was full of concern for me.

She put out the light and we got into bed. She came over to give me a goodnight kiss. Her kiss immediately plunged me into slumber. My day had worn me out.

It could have been about three o'clock in the morning when a nightmare woke me up. I cried out. . . . Terrifying visions. . . . My father was trying to catch me, people were running behind me on the quayside, I was trying in vain to reach a hand which was stretched out to me, far in the distance. Aunt Maria held me in her arms, to calm me down. She whispered a few words to me in the darkness. My head rested in the hollow of her breasts, and she held me tightly to her. I breathed in her scent, the warmth of her body forming a safe haven, and her legs tenderly enfolding me. This was something completely unfamiliar to me. The visions and images disappeared, giving way to others. Images of a childhood devoid of maternal tenderness. Much later – *dear comrade* – I shall recall that moment.'

Reinaldo stopped and bought me another drink. He patted me on the shoulder as a sign of friendship. I was his *comrade* for the night, listening to his confession. As his story progressed, his face was transformed. His changing expressions, in the softly filtered light of the club, punctuated each period of his life. He relived his past and constantly mimed each stage of his adventure:

'Reinaldo, surely you're not going to make me

believe that the sensual and voluble Aunt Maria left you with such scant memories?'

'That's true. The crossing was long and Aunt Maria had several surprises in store for me,' he replied, and then took up his story once again.

'Aunt Maria caressed my head, then I felt her hand running down the length of my body. Her silk night-gown clung to her body and I rested my arm on the magnificent swell of her backside. I had scarcely emerged from my nightmare. She had strange ways and was rubbing my torso. We did not say a word. The silence of the night hung heavy. The boat was pitching a little. She whispered incomprehensible words, as though she were trying to calm a child. Suddenly she lifted herself up to check if I was asleep. My eyes were closed, giving the impression that I had gone back to sleep. She smoothed her hand across my forehead and ran it through my hair. She laid herself down right next to me again and began to caress my thighs, my buttocks. I did not move. Then she placed her hand on my lower belly and moved downwards, very slowly. She was afraid of waking me. She felt for my penis. I felt her hand approaching and covering it. It felt hot. Her body seemed to vibrate. My penis unbent little by little. Then I realized that she was lifting her nightgown up around her belly. I was on the alert for her slightest movement. She drew close again. Her warm belly, her soft skin and her pubis rubbed my thigh with a slow, deep rhythm. She moved her arms and took hold of her breasts to knead them. She gave little muffled moans, and her breathing became quicker. Then, in a single movement, she pressed herself even harder against me as she masturbated herself. I heard her moaning and biting her fingers. She caressed my prick once more and then pulled down her nightgown.

She took me in her arms and once again lodged my head between her heavy breasts whose pointed tips nudged against my mouth. Her heart was beating wildly. But I fell asleep and slumbered on till morning without waking.

Aunt Maria got up first. She was wearing a turquoise blue dressing-gown. As soon as I opened my eyes I saw her: she was doing her hair. She turned round and asked me if I'd spent a good night with her. She confessed that she had a spot of backache this morning, having slept in an awkward position in that bunk which was too narrow for two. She showed me where it hurt and uncovered her shoulders. She then wanted me to massage her. She lay down and took off her dressing-gown, keeping on her nightgown. She uncovered her upper back and bust. Her breasts were as beautiful as those of her nieces. They were heavier, but stood proud like two sculptures on her chest. I went up to her and she handed me some cream, showing me where I should massage. The session lasted ten minutes. When she stood up, she was not in the least embarrassed at showing me her breasts. She gave me a vague smile as she saw me following her movements as she got dressed.

She went to see if Carlotta and Yolanda were awake. But they were still asleep. She gave me some fruit, promising me a more substantial meal later on.

Yolanda and Carlotta arrived half an hour later, excited by what had happened. Aunt Maria calmed them and ordered them to get on with breakfast. They did so quickly, returning with a tray of milk, coffee, rolls and fruit. After this interlude, the day had to be organized, my movements had to be planned, and everything done to prevent my being noticed. Aunt Maria volunteered to go and buy me some clothes in the shop on the boat. There wasn't much choice. She bought me a fashionable pair of swimming trunks, a short-sleeved shirt and a pair of trousers. The girls offered me sandals and socks. I was happy.

The first days were all very similar. I swam in the pool with Carlotta and Yolanda, when the passengers all crowded in at the same time. In this way I stood less chance of being noticed and I avoided the crew-members who might have asked me questions. Aunt Maria spent her days with her musician friend. They often met in the bar where there was a badly tuned but playable piano.

Carlotta and Yolanda acted as my bodyguards. But they were real rogues. Sometimes they wanted me to wait for them for several hours in the cabin. Or they took turns at keeping me company, playing cards with me or inventing more exciting games. It was a way of passing the time. During the daytime, we mixed with the passengers in the bar and had a few nibbles there. There was also a gaming room but we didn't spend much time in there. The place was too dangerous, because crew-members often met up there.

On the second evening, Yolanda and Carlotta wanted me to stay in their cabin. They had to persuade their aunt that this should happen. They found the solution. After dinner, we had begun a game which they had brought with them. When Aunt Maria arrived around eleven o'clock, she could see that we were completely absorbed in this parlour-game. She asked us if we were going to be long. Yolanda replied that she had no idea and that if it went on longer than expected, I could sleep here. Aunt Maria made great play of the embarrassment they might feel if I were to stay there and sleep with them. I didn't know what to say. She was giving me looks loaded with meaning. I looked at her with respect, admiring her beauty. She must have understood. Because of that, she agreed to leave me with Yolanda and Carlotta. She asked the girls to be good and not make too much noise. Yolanda and Carlotta kissed her and Aunt Maria gave me a kiss, advising me not to have another nightmare. The girls looked at me in astonishment. Then, when their aunt went out, they questioned me. I told them everything. Except for the episode of her touching me. But they undoubtedly suspected as much.

The days and evenings seemed interminable to me. Yet Yolanda did everything she could to make me feel a part of their little family. We often embraced. Carlotta, who was more of a hussy, if not an expert, touched me up incessantly. Her sister wanted to do the same and, without asking my opinion, would take hold of my hand and guide it to her chest. Her breasts reminded me of Aunt Maria's. I began to enjoy their games. I relaxed in this game of caresses whilst Carlotta went into the bathroom to freshen up. Yolanda took off my short-sleeved shirt and unbuttoned my trousers, whilst giving me a lingering kiss. I caressed her breasts and tried to unhook her bodice. But I couldn't really manage it.

She helped me and was soon naked, her breasts pressed up against my chest. She began to murmur words in my ear. Desire made me deaf. I wanted to make love to her madly, distractedly. I realized that I was supposed to lick her beautiful juicy water-melons. That's what her sister called them. Yolanda compared hers to Brazilian mangoes.

Carlotta came out of the bathroom and caught us unawares. She switched off the light and threw herself on top of us with a cry of joy. She asked us to wait for her. Yolanda moved away to allow Carlotta to undress me completely. I offered no resistance. Carlotta covered me with kisses, and caressed me all over. We rolled on to the floor. Yolanda joined us. They clung to me, rubbing their thighs up against mine. Carlotta began to play with my prick. She caressed it to make it grow between her fingers. Then she laid herself down on me and tried to stick it up inside her cunt. She was using me like a tool. This phenomenon excited me enormously, for it was the first time it had ever happened to me. Carlotta gave me all the necessary advice. The opening was small and the pressure was painful. The excitement mounted, I moved my belly and, with a violent thrust of my lower back, I penetrated her. She pushed down hard and took me into her. She was frantic, excited, unrestrained. She found relief. Now she was moving up and down on top of me. She gave me a few more snippets of advice. It all seemed unreal to me, for Yolanda was caressing me whilst her sister took her pleasure. Mine was not going to be long in coming. Carlotta realized this. She pulled away from me and took hold of my prick and handled it as vigorously as she could until it burst forth in her hand. She took a twofold pleasure in the liquid which flooded all over her.

I was stretched out full-length, looking up at the ceiling. Yolanda came close to me and took my hand. Carlotta brought a towel to wipe myself with and planted a kiss on my belly. The touch of her mouth made me start, whilst Yolanda laid her head in the crook of my shoulder. I was aroused once again. Yolanda was romantic, and we exchanged many kisses. Her tongue twisted about in my mouth, which pleased me enormously. I slid my hand towards her pubis and began to take her in hand. She tried to get a grip on herself, stifling her breathing in my neck. I rolled about on the ground with her. She burst out laughing. Carlotta pleaded with us to keep the noise down.

Carlotta directed our frolics and urged her to give me great pleasure. Yolanda would not allow me to penetrate her. I respected her wishes, but she wanted to be forgiven. She moved down to the level of my belly, then seized hold of my prick which she caressed with little jerky movements. She ordered me to close my eyes and I felt her putting my prick into her mouth. This surprised me – the sensation was soft and sweet, smooth and mellow. Her tongue slid over my prick, and I could sense that she was greatly enjoying sucking me. My head was spinning. I was hard in her mouth. I wondered if I should hold myself back. I felt as though I was about to join the angels in Paradise. My hands rested on her head. My body had contracted and I placed wet kisses on her mouth, her face. She drew away and rubbed her face on my belly. I caressed her head and drew her to me, first touching and then kissing her breasts. We revelled in our silent pleasure. Each of us had escaped from the other in a bubble where there was no more reality, no sounds, no words, no indiscreet looks. Even Carlotta respected our dizzy intertwinings, our awkward movements, our adolescent hesitations. Carlotta was asleep, or pretending to be. I stayed like that, entwined with Yolanda. I heard a noise without knowing where it came from.

Later on, I found out that someone had opened the cabin door. That's another story, *dear comrade*, which I shall tell you in detail.

I spent the night like that with Yolanda, in her bunk. In the early morning, they awoke me quickly before Aunt Maria arrived. I put on my clothes. I waited until the girls had had a wash before I rinsed my face. My razor was in their aunt's cabin. At last we were ready when Aunt Maria came to collect them for breakfast. She asked if we had had a good night and asked Yolanda a second time. Yolanda and Carlotta seemed embarrassed. I behaved as if I hadn't heard anything, whilst still being polite to her.

These mornings were the most painful. Sometimes I had to stay locked away. Then I read illustrated magazines and the papers that were given out on the boat. Carlotta and Yolanda had a few books, but they didn't interest me much. The waiting became painful. I would pace up and down aimlessly in the cabin. For a moment, I felt a strong desire to go for a walk round the boat without asking Aunt Maria's opinion. I wanted to explore the keelson, which was not very big. There were about a hundred or so passengers, according to what the girls said. That's why it was better if I didn't make an appearance.

This new day was just like the previous one. Aunt Maria fussed about us warmly. She often laughed with her two nieces and teased them. I didn't dare risk any familiarity with Yolanda and Carlotta in their aunt's presence. But she must have suspected how intimate we had become. To Aunt Maria, I was a child – albeit a child who had grown up very quickly.

In the evening, she brought some provisions to me in her nieces' cabin. All three of us were quite tired, and Aunt Maria asked the girls to go to bed without too much delay. She told them that I would spend the night in her cabin: it was better that way. Carlotta, the elder girl, was lost for a reply.

And so I followed Aunt Maria.

She went into the bathroom and turned on the shower-spray. Suddenly, she called me in to check if the water was warm enough. I hesitated for a moment, and she repeated her request. I hurried in and saw she was wearing a dressing-gown, which revealed her breasts and gaped open to show her abundant thighs. She displayed herself in a leisurely fashion. She talked to me about the day's events whilst I regulated the temperature of the water. She said she hadn't found the people she'd met very interesting, and that I was lucky to have Carlotta and Yolanda to entertain me . . . I wondered what she was getting at. I interrupted her to tell her that the water was at the right temperature. She put on her shower-cap, took off her dressing-gown and gave it to me to hang it up. I averted my eyes, avoiding her naked body, and was about to leave the shower when she invited me to stay and rub her back. She continued to talk to me about one thing and another, but I wasn't listening any more.

Her nudity disturbed me. She was beautiful, and was offering me the thousand luxuriant treasures of her body. The broad expanse of her buttocks made me shiver; the curving fall of her backside cried out to be caressed; the perfect roundness of her breasts drew my gaze, provoking a desire to snuggle between these two domes of warmth. I followed her words, punctuating them constantly with an acquiescent *si Señora*. She said that I could call her Aunt Maria. I fell in with her wishes. I could refuse her nothing; she was as magical as a statue of the Madonna.

I tried to keep track of the conversation, whilst pretending to be indifferent to the fascinating spectacle she was treating me to. As she moved about and rubbed herself, she drew slow, sinuous lines in the water. The soap slid over her amber, suntanned skin. She turned round and handed me the sponge. In a state of total confusion, I ran it over her upper and lower back, and then over her buttocks, as she wished. As I was clumsy, she often reproved me. Next, she let me get undressed and insisted that I had a shower. When I was alone, I dried myself and put on my pyjama jacket, keeping my underpants on. I went out of the shower and found Aunt Maria stretched out on her bunk in the half-darkness.

She asked me to switch off the last light, then come over and kiss her. Whilst I was bending over her, she pulled me vigorously towards her and made space for me next to her. It was then that she asked me: 'You really like Yolanda, don't you? What did you do together yesterday evening..?' I blurted out a few confused words. I was overcome by a feeling of discomfort. She told me that I was a big boy now, and that I had to know about the facts of life and what people call love. There was nothing shameful about making it, she insisted. But she wanted to teach me these things according to the rules of the game. Aunt Maria, enticing Maria, that sensual and explosive Venezuelan, taught me voluptuous kisses, spicy caresses, ways to suck the very best parts of the body, the charms of each millimetre of a woman's skin, those of the folds of her body when it was convulsed by pleasure. She guided my penis, as her niece Carlotta had done, into her deep, wet cunt. Because of my youth, I was able to have several erections with Maria. In the course of that illustrious night, she succeeded in exhausting me and, at the same time, began my sexual education. Aunt Maria was the first sex-bomb I had ever met. I spent that exceptional night in silence, whilst Maria sang her entire repertoire of pleasure: whispers, piercing and low-pitched cries, incomprehensible words, music voiced in the dizzy intoxication I was discovering.

Next morning, she awoke me after she had got herself ready. Yolanda and Carlotta came and shook me awake in my bed; Aunt Maria let them do so cheerfully and not without malice. We ate guavas, papayas and mangoes.

The crossing proceeded at the same rhythm for a week. Sometimes I was with Yolanda and Carlotta in their cabin or at the pool, and sometimes I was with Aunt Maria.

Matters became more complicated the day when Aunt Maria told me that it was no longer possible to conceal my presence on board. We were too often seen together on deck or in the bar. The ship's captain was beginning to get to know all his passengers and, each evening at dinner, he liked to greet a few of the groups of guests sitting at the tables by buying them a drink. She was afraid that he might pay her a visit at any moment. Each evening she left her table hurriedly, sending her nieces back to join me. Aunt Maria usually played the piano in the bar for a while, and went back to her cabin after her walk on deck.

Yolanda and Carlotta tried to find a solution. But their aunt persuaded them not to do anything rash.

I noticed that Aunt Maria was beginning to fear the complexity of the situation in which she had placed herself. She was not deceived by the double game being played between us and her nieces. She was looking for alternative fates for me. I didn't delude myself any longer. I counted the passing days, and that helped me to damp down my anguish. From now on, I wasn't going to think about anything except getting to Spain.

My story began to take a difficult turn.

On the evening when Aunt Maria was asking herself a thousand questions to help her come to a decision about me, I slept in her nieces' cabin. They had become jealous of their aunt and showed me so with a rare competency. They began to dance a *bambuco* for me – a Colombian dance which was popular throughout Latin America. They offered me sweetmeats during the daytime, and in the evening prepared my dinner. That night, they ran riot, hoping to please me. Carlotta began to do a sort of old-fashioned striptease, imitating the professionals in her own way. At the same time, she sang an old popular song:

> White I was born, and I shall tell
> The reason why I've dusky grown.
> You see, I love the sun so well
> That my pale skin has turned quite brown.

Yolanda roared with laughter, whilst I applauded the extravagant Carlotta. She hurled her clothes into the air and threw her bra in my face. Yolanda, who was more modest by nature, turned down the lights and wisely locked the cabin door. Carlotta then urged her to do a dance in my honour. Carlotta sat down next to me and caressed me. She had taken off her nightgown, patterned with little purple and yellow flowers. Yolanda did an Indian dance, mixed up with movements from Latin-American folk-dances. She ended by pointing her toes and doing classical arabesques. We applauded her enthusiastically, then I kissed her tenderly on both cheeks. Yolanda had the gift of unsettling me, and my gestures became awkward.

But that wasn't all that happened that night, *dear comrade*.

The girls asked me openly what their Aunt Maria had taught me in her bunk. For a moment I pretended to be astonished. Carlotta tried to worm it out of me by coaxing me sexually. Yolanda waited in silence for me to reveal secrets. I asked her to put out the lights.

When all three of us were undressed, I went to work on Yolanda by sucking the tips of her breasts. Carlotta pressed herself up against me and took my hand, directing it towards her breasts whilst with the other I caressed her pubis, working my way gradually between her labia as Aunt Maria had advised me. Yolanda moved under the weight of my mouth which was biting her breasts and making her wet. Carlotta found my caresses effective, and called me a rogue.

I was wanking her harder and harder. Yolanda wanted me to enter her, but she begged me not be brutal. Carlotta moved away, satisfied, and left me alone with her sister. Yolanda was as wet as her aunt. I had no difficulty in burying my prick in her. I pushed in and out of her, sometimes slowly, sometimes rapidly. She became tense, then relaxed; then gave a powerful thrust of her hips so that we became one body, moving to the same rhythm. I felt her literally melting with pleasure. Her breathing was faster, she gripped my prick as hard as she could and gave out an immense sigh. The trembling of her hips and belly produced an electric effect at the base of my prick. I felt the liquid rising and pulled out at the last second. Carlotta seemed ready, and I invited her to take me into her mouth. That was indeed what she wanted. She sucked me assiduously – perhaps she was unconsciously imitating her aunt? – and swallowed me right down her throat. Droplets glistened on her mouth. When I withdrew I was completely sated. I stretched out on the floor with my arms folded. Yolanda and Carlotta surrounded me tenderly. All three of us lay there side by side, giving each other a myriad kisses, naturally and romantically.

When I got up next morning, I was stiff all over. I had slept on the floor on thin blankets, so as not to disturb Yolanda in her bunk. The experiment was not a successful one. The girls massaged my back and I had to move about a bit to relax my muscles.

That day was not like the previous ones. Aunt Maria arrived around ten am. Her face seemed tense, her dark eyes reflecting a feeling of sorrow, and she was less talkative than usual. She kissed me very tenderly. Yolanda enquired about her state. Aunt Maria gave a vague wave of the hand, signifying that it was nothing. Carlotta remained silent.

The girls left with their aunt. I remained alone in the cabin, waiting for an opportune moment to take the air on deck with the girls. The wait, which seemed exceptionally long to me, passed as though I were in a dream. What's more, I fell asleep and slumbered on until I was suddenly awoken.

Usually it was Carlotta and Yolanda who came to let me know that I could go out. I waited for them as my supreme deliverance. When I opened my eyes, I felt someone shaking me. Aunt Maria was bending over me, her face twisted with discomfort. She put an abrupt end to my sleepiness. I leapt up and, without saying a word, she took me by the hand, into the corridor, where she spoke to me in serious tones.

She had decided to take me to see the ship's captain, as it was no longer possible to hide me. She was responsible for her nieces and could no longer put up with this illicit situation. Sooner or later, I would have come face to face with the captain and customs procedures. All of this had to be sorted out. She was almost weeping as she painted the picture of what awaited me. I was now speechless, and fell in with every word she said. She apologized many times, kissing me all over my forehead. The tears which I felt welling up burned my eyes, but I managed to suppress them. I remembered that Aunt Maria, adorable Maria, had told me that I was now a man. I wanted to behave like one to the bitter end. And before all the authorities!

We went to the captain's office, which was not far from the navigation room, on the topmost part of the boat, opposite the swimming-pool.

The man who faced me smelt of alcohol. He was fat and wore a horrible moustache. His uniform was unbuttoned and his manners were not exactly deferential.

Aunt Maria introduced me to him. He began to shout, but I heard absolutely nothing. When he asked Maria to go out and leave him alone with me, I at last heard his voice clearly. Aunt Maria squeezed my hand, which she had not let go of. I watched her close the door on us.

The captain asked me a thousand questions all at once. I didn't know how to reply. He threatened to throw me to the sharks: that was his right as captain, he told me. Then he calmed down, seeing that I was not flinching. His first question led me to tell him why I had taken this boat. I told him that I wanted to get to Spain. I didn't have enough money for the journey, as my father had abandoned me with friends whilst he was working in Colombia, at Bogota. I couldn't wait any longer for him to return. At that moment, the captain asked me where my mother was. I gave him a partial explanation of the situation. She had left my father and I wanted to find her. That was the sole aim of my journey. Moreover, I no longer wanted to live in Venezuela or join my father in Bogota.

The captain then told me that I must pay for my journey in one way or another, before we got to Spain. Then at Santa Cruz de Tenerife, I would have to obtain a passport and an entry visa. He was not sure that that would be possible. All his gabblings were incomprehensible to me.

He took a decision. I would help to clean the dining rooms and the cabins. Next, he would find me a place to sleep without inconveniencing the lady who had sheltered me. At the end of this interview, he opened the door and explained everything to Aunt Maria who was waiting for me with Yolanda and Carlotta. I walked out and went to collect my things.

Now, I was seen everywhere. I put on a uniform to carry out my duties for a few hours during the day and before dinner. I spent my leisure hours with Yolanda and Carlotta at the pool. The nights continued to be surprising. I went to Aunt Maria's cabin when she wanted me to, and then to the girls' cabin where we had a grand time.

It only remained for me to go through the ordeal of arriving at Santa Cruz de Tenerife.

Five days after being discovered as a stowaway, I arrived in that port. The authorities were alerted to my presence on board the *Estrellita*.

I left Yolanda, Carlotta and Aunt Maria, beautiful Maria who had opened the secret doors of her body to me and shown me the first rites of love. Nor shall I forget the games which I had shared with her two nieces. My heart had pounded faster for Yolanda especially.

Now I was to have other cares. At Santa Cruz de Tenerife, the authorities did not provide me with a visa. I couldn't stay any longer than the boat, which was continuing its journey towards Spain. I asked if I could work in the port. The customs department entrusted me to the port authorities. Above all, I had to find some money so that I could get to Spain.

In those days, there weren't so many visitors to the Canary Isles. Las Palmas became a holiday centre in the Sixties. Santa Cruz was opposite it. During the few hours I spent reflecting on my situation, I felt a desire to go there. I might perhaps have a better chance of getting to Spain if I went via Morocco. Submissively, I put myself in the hands of the authorities who had tried to contact the Venezuelan Consulate to tell them where I was. A solution was found which would give me work and provide me with papers before I embarked once more for Spain.

I did clerical work for the customs for more than a fortnight. By the evening, I was completely exhausted, but – because I wanted to earn a little more money – I took to washing dishes in a bar. I slept in an inn which was popular with foreigners, and where passengers planning to make their way to Spain were to be found.

I should tell you, *dear comrade*, that I had lied to the authorities by telling them that I was eighteen. It made it less complicated to work things out.

My first nights in Santa Cruz, under the pressure of events, had turned me into an insomniac. Fear, the anguish of not achieving my goals, tortured me. Each evening, to calm myself down, I took the yellowed photo of my mother out of my pocket.'

'All through my voyage to Spain my mother's eyes accompanied me. They supported me. Thanks to my mother, I persevered and, in spite of the vicissitudes of the journey, I came gradually closer to my goal. So I boarded the boat again, paying for my berth in a modest cabin. The captain allowed me to carry out certain tasks to earn myself a little nest-egg for when I set foot on Spanish soil.

During this crossing, I got to know many Spaniards and, notably a lady who was always alone, wandering about the ship, with a wild look in her eyes. The captain introduced me to her and told her about my situation. This woman had just lost her husband. She had no children. Her name was well known in her country. Her husband had been high up in the civil service. She was returning to Cadiz after a long journey. Once there, she was going to go back to a big, empty house, lands and a fortune which was too extensive to count, according to what the captain said.

I disembarked at Cadiz with Doña Gloria Villanueva

de Montero. She took care of the formalities and asked for me to be given asylum in Spain. She adopted me as though I were an orphan. I had had time to get to know her better during the last three days of the crossing. She spent her day reading a very old 1902 edition of Saint Ignatius Loyola's *Spiritual Exercises* – a book bound in mauve leather – which included a note, a sort of foreword for the salvation of souls, written by the Cardinal of Burgos. She lent me this mystical book, whose tone intrigued me. I understood none of it. Later, she told me that she had known the Cardinal of Burgos when she was a child. When I saw her for the first time, she was wearing a veil over her face. She scarcely took it off during the whole journey. I could only guess at her features. We left the port together, and got into a car which was waiting for her. It was when we arrived at her estate, near San Fernando, that she at last took off her veil, as well as her hat and spectacles.

She had a broad forehead, black hair drawn back, a long, slender nose, and grey eyes with black-rimmed irises, which gave her the look of a cat. Under her linen mourning dress, I could make out rounded hips, fleshy thighs. Her bosom seemed abnormally compressed. But she held herself very upright, which I took to be a sign of pride.

She asked her household servant to get her bedroom ready, as well as mine. Later on, we had a snack together. This gave me an opportunity to get a better look at her. My eyes met her smile, filled with grace and understanding. We talked of education.

And what an education! From time to time, I was still nonplussed. She devoted herself to prayer, and had a wickerwork prie-dieu in the dressing-room which led to her bedroom. I often saw her at prayer. Sometimes I heard her chanting in the distance. When that happened, the old woman who worked for her took her head in her hands as a sign of deep affliction. I knew no more than that.

The days and weeks passed.

It was summer. She spent most of her time alone. I came and went with the old woman who cared for her, who showed me the sights of San Fernando when she went out on her numerous errands. I also went to Cadiz to swim and walk among the little back-streets. I was very much attracted by music, and often spent the latter part of the afternoons listening to musicians and singers near the inns. In the evening, I went back on the bus.

She delayed dinner until I got back, so that I could tell her about my day. She was getting used to me and I was getting used to her. The heat was stifling; she settled herself on the patio with her books. I recognized the one she had shown me on the boat, but she also read novels. She advised me to do some reading and I selected a few books from her husband's library. During these summer days, she modified her severe style of dress. She wore light dresses in pastel

45

shades. The lines of her body rippled and her movements were more relaxed. Sometimes I could see sadness in her furrowed brow, or a certain degree of seriousness would manifest itself when she read *Spiritual Exercises*. She walked along with her book in her hand and crossed herself frequently. When she disappeared into the house, I could hear her ranting wildly. The old serving-woman explained to me that she was bemoaning her fate, that she wanted to impose penances upon herself. She was an ascetic; she believed that she was a sinner and was now throwing herself into the *path of salvation*.

Doña Gloria, my protector, gave her old servant a holiday, and she left for several weeks at the beginning of August. I remained alone with her, and helped her with the household chores. So I came into contact with her more frequently, and began to get to know her better. She set aside times for her reflections. She spoke openly of her past life, and the status she had held in relation to her husband. Now she wanted to devote herself to charitable works, or at least, that was her intention.

But her last intention, *dear comrade*, was to prepare herself for interior and external meditation. For that she needed a framework to her life and a motive force quite different from her precious *Exercises*! After adopting me, she used me to provide her with support in her very own brand of prayers and her different ceremonies, designed to purify her past life. She began by shutting herself away and praying intensely. Her meals became more and more sparse (though she prepared mine without any change from normal). One morning, after waking me up, she told me that in that very first week of August she was going to begin her penance and that she would certainly need my services – however minimal they might be!

Doña Gloria prepared me by lending me a prayer-book, then she left her favourite book, *Spiritual Exercises*, on the bedside table in my room! I scanned it before going to sleep, and found the notes on the general self-examination which the penitent must carry out and – the part which is more to the point in the case of Doña Gloria – the extraordinary *weeks* designed to purify the soul and body: these were divided into numbered days, from five to twelve. A real programme! I couldn't understand how she was going to arrange things so that I could play a part in her meditation.

I was on the patio when I heard heart-rending cries punctuated with periods of silence. These cries were coming from Doña Gloria's room. I walked towards the house. The cries rang out again. I went up to the first floor, walking very softly. The cries were indeed coming from her. I approached the door, which was half-open. To my great surprise, I saw her whipping her bosom with leather thongs. She took off her bodice and hit herself again several times, with little control but plenty of force. Her cries followed fragments of prayer. She held herself upright, her face turned towards the pious picture which decorated one of her bedroom walls. I saw her back contract, and watched her arms moving, making her hips sway and uncovering her heavy breasts, bruised by the blows. I averted my gaze and walked away.

The sight of Doña Gloria aroused me for a short moment. But immediately I drove it from my mind. At the moment when I was about to step back on to the patio, I heard someone calling me. I hesitated before replying; I went out and made a noise so that she would hear me coming back. She was on her prie-dieu, fully clothed, her bodice tightly buttoned and a thick belt around her waist. When I reached her room, she spoke with her back to me. Her penance had begun. She turned towards me and said:

'Reinaldo, the first day of the First Week is the hardest. Contemplation is the first step, but I must feel the pain of my sins. My body must suffer and I must experience repentence in my flesh . . . I do not have four arms. Take these leather thongs and beat my shoulders and back, please.'

On her face I could discern affliction, tiredness and remorse. I became disconcerted. Not a sound passed my lips. All this time she was staring at me and I felt terribly embarrassed when she challenged me by turning her eyes towards the thongs which were lying beside her. Then I picked them up. And I hit her a few times, clumsily. She insisted that I must hit her harder. Which I did, though I felt extremely confused and disturbed.

Her bodice was beginning to give way under the

blows. She unbuttoned it then bared her shoulders. Her head jolted and bowed forward. I stopped for a moment but she ordered me to begin again. Her voice was distorted by suffering. She belched out incomprehensible words. And she tore off her bodice violently, baring her back to me. Her breasts were bandaged up with a strip of rough sacking, which compressed her bosom. After a quarter of an hour, she swayed on her prie-dieu and fell. I rushed to her and supported her. She was delirious. Her face looked at me as though she were in ecstasy, with a slight smile at the corners of her mouth. I carried her across to the bed.

She had the strength to thank me. I was aghast. She guided my hand to the bandage and I realized that I must take it off. I obeyed. Her insistent gaze chilled me. Her breasts were pinkish, the areolae dilated and the nipples hard. Her heart was leaping about in her chest. I went to get her a glass of water. She refused it, saying: 'Not now!' Hearing her speak made me feel better. She took my hand again and guided it to her chest, closing her eyes. She massaged her breasts with my hand, slowly. I followed her movements carefully. I felt myself weakening. Disgust and pleasure were mingling within me. My prick became erect and I was ashamed of it. But I caressed her breasts with great pleasure. She pushed one hand away and drew me towards her bosom. Her eyes were still closed. She offered only one word: 'Come!' I was already on top of her, lying against her breasts, with my head nuzzling between them. She sought my mouth with her fingers and guided it towards her breasts. Anxiously I followed her movements. Then I sucked her hardened nipples and caressed her hips in long strokes. She moaned as though to release herself. Then she became delirious. I realized that she was being overcome by pleasure. She gave a laugh of pleasure and her face was bathed in the strangest look of blessedness. She twisted about under my caresses and was at last sated. She gave a long sigh. I climbed off the bed, got a glass of water, lifted her head and tried to make her drink. I managed it, not without considerable difficulty. Now she seemed to be falling asleep.

I turned her on to her belly to see if her back was still marked. Her flesh had acknowledged the blows: there were three red lines. I took a linen towel from the bathroom and applied it to her back. I covered her up and went out, completely exhausted by this episode.

When I got into bed that evening, I once again picked up the little book which she had placed in my room. I opened it at the beginning of those famous *Exercises* and realized that Doña Gloria's interpretation of them went beyond the plan for her penance. I closed it again after reading the first notes concerning corporal punishment. The point was to prepare the soul by getting rid of all of one's unruly affections. It seemed to me that Doña Gloria had stretched the rules!

During the night, I went into her bedroom. She

was sleeping. Once again I refilled her glass of water and left it on the bedside table. I covered her with a blanket. The images of her pain troubled me again, then they disappeared. I thought of her body, her breasts which I had liberated.

It took me a long time to get to sleep.

In the morning, Doña Gloria did not wake me as she usually did. I went into the kitchen where everything was laid out for breakfast. I found a message in which she told me that she was going into town. Later on, I noticed that she had cleaned the downstairs rooms. The patio had been newly watered and so had the orchard. The vegetables had been picked and were arranged in a large basket.

That day, I decided to look at the books which she had got out for me. I found Spanish and Italian mystical anthologies. I saw novels too. One of them aroused my curiosity: *Misericordia*. I read a few pages of it, and also opened *Divinas palabras*, which was about a strangely eccentric Don Juan. Perhaps Doña Gloria stimulated her imagination with these books in order to relax after her *Exercises*.

I waited like a caged bird for her return.

She arrived, weighed down with shopping, late in the afternoon. I helped her to carry the various parcels and she asked me to put one of them in her bedroom. It might perhaps have contained underwear. She made absolutely no mention of the previous night, or of the troubles she had undergone. I too remained tight-lipped on that subject. When I came back from her

51

bedroom she smiled at me for a long time; I joined her in the kitchen where she had laid out vegetables, fruit and other foodstuffs.

Then I went to the drawing-room and pretended to read whilst she was getting the meal ready. Afterwards, she went up to her room and I heard the sound of running water.

She came back down dressed in red and black. Her face was radiant. Her expression had changed. She went into the kitchen. The table was already laid. She brought in the dishes and, after evening prayers, we began to eat with gusto.

Dinner over, she cleared the table. She asked me to wait for her in the reading-room and said she would bring in two cups of herbal tea. She wanted me to read the book which she had recommended to me. In fact, I was to participate in her penance by knowing how it would unfold that night. I then read what was involved in the first *week*, and the *second* day of Doña Gloria's life of contemplation. It was more eccentric that her mystical books suggested.

Night fell. And Doña Gloria went up to the first floor after drinking her herb tea. When I went up to my room, she was already in hers. I lay down on the bed – and drifted off into an absurd reverie.

I heard the sound of unwrapping coming from her room. Objects which jingled fell on to the floor. I couldn't tell what they were. A few minutes later, I heard her voice. She was beginning her prayers. I began to listen intently. As though coming from far away, the sound of moaning rose and filled the house. These were no longer cries, this was like a moment of pleasure which, *in extremis*, comes out of pain. Out of a body which experiences joy in the midst of torment. What was Doña Gloria indulging in?

She took harsh measures to deal with her body.

When she called me in to join her, I was surprised to find her surrounded by the most unusual apparatus. Doña Gloria had unwrapped the parcel which I had taken into her large bedroom. There were ropes, leather thongs, different sorts of whips, little chains. On her prie-dieu, two bricks occupied the place where her knees rested, and the whole of the surface of her bed was covered by a thin wooden board. There were also two ladders, leaning against the wall. Candles on two candelabra spread a feeble light through the room. A muted, filtered light as though for a very peculiar and, at the same time, very sophisticated place of worship. I had not seen her setting up what constituted the regalia of her penance – a penance which also consisted of experiencing pleasure.

She was wearing different clothes: a one-piece, knee-length dress. I didn't really notice what she was wearing round her waist. She raised her voice and said that tonight her body must know 'a great austerity'. She wished to overcome herself completely. She confided in me as though she feared a change of heart or a refusal from me.

She gave me a sort of monk's habit. Then she showed me various silken cords. She went and stood

53

against the wall, in between the two ladders which seemed to be fixed there. She asked me to tie her there with outstretched arms, outspread legs, and to criss-cross two cords between her breasts and her shoulders. In this way, her two breasts were parted and stood free on her torso. She began to say prayers. Then she turned towards me and, giving me a sign, asked me to pick up the leather thongs which were in a bag. Whilst I was getting ready, she spoke mysterious phrases: 'I shall, on the contrary, try always to maintain the desire to experience pain and repentance. . . .' Now I had to carry out my task. And the leather thongs came lashing down upon her body. She continued to give me specific instructions as to the different parts which I should attack. Her eyes were lost in a penitential violence which tore intestinal rumblings, little shrill cries and grotesque laughter from her.

I did not hit her hard. But her confusion was so great that she played with the pain she imagined she felt. Then I began to feel sexual impulses. Her little dress was tearing as she twisted about. Her flesh revealed itself to me in the ochre-coloured light of the bedroom. Her straining breasts were tossed about and almost leapt out of their silken yoke. Her tongue played across her lips, and her thighs moved further apart as her pelvis moved about frantically.

This was the first part of the theatrical production. The second part was carried out with litanies and orders which she gave me. I had to carry them out. I was anxious, for her cries were echoing through that big house.

I then laid her down on the board which covered the bed. I tied her up more firmly than before. She made me hold out my left hand, first of all, so that I could whip her as she wished me to. The right hand would play its part later on, to coax her flesh. I tore off her dress and she was completely naked. She advised me to use the little chains so that her body could not move away, so that it could not extricate itself from its suffering. I gave way to her desires; not without emotion.

Her belly contracted when she felt the chains. Her chest inflated, I saw her breasts leaping forward and I waited for the moment she she would allow me to take hold of them. My body was exploding under my monastic outfit. Her skin was gleaming with sweat and her scent went to my head. I did not know how to hold myself back any longer. It was at that moment that she said to me: 'Your lance! Your carnal lance must run me through! Come, crucify me! . . .' With my lance erect, I melted into her, taking hold of her hips to hold her up. Her rhythm drove me crazy. Her face shone brightly and she babbled incessantly. I laid my body against hers, marrying together our most secret places. In a moment I released her. Her voice became softer, as though veiled by pleasure, I unfastened her hands and feet which had not been hurt in any way. She began to lick all the damp places on my body, moved up my thighs and took my carnal lance with a mystic devotion. She was racked with spasms as I exerted a smooth pressure on her heavy, straining breasts. She sucked me with an angelic gentleness.

As the night progressed, she made infernal demands on me. She wanted me to take her on her prie-dieu after beating her with the thongs. Then she begged me to tie her between the two ladders, with her head turned to the wall.

She presented her outspread buttocks to me: her legs trembled, dancing lightly. During all her exercised, she never stopped talking and giving me instructions. I rubbed her between her buttocks, and caressed her pubis, before sliding into her with my hard lance, whilst I masturbated her violently. Her orgasms succeeded each other at a furious pace. Although I was worn out, I hastened her pleasure with my hand; she collapsed with a terrible cry with paralysed me. She too made no further movement. This was the signal for me to carry her to the bed and disappear until the next morning.

Doña Gloria woke up early the next morning and organized absolutely everything. What surprised me right from the early days was her ability to forget what she asked of me during her nights of penance and pleasure. Her body never carried a mark to show the violent acts she imposed upon herself, and each day her face became a little more radiant. My mornings were taken over by her devastating charm and she was full of attentions for me. Her widowhood became for her a springboard to another life. Now I belonged to her rites, her spiritual and bodily ceremonial.

At certain times of day, I tried to avoid her. I went off into the hills. She left me free to move about as I pleased. Sometimes I asked her if I could go to San Fernando or Cadiz for a swim. She told me not to dawdle and to get back by seven o'clock for the evening meal. I never went against her wishes.

Each evening, I couldn't wait to find out how Doña Gloria was progressing in her endeavours.

On the third evening, she said her prayers and told me that she was going to bed early as a long journey awaited her the next day. I didn't know what it was all about.

She accompanied me to my room and kissed me on the forehead before going back to her own room. I heard her going to bed. And I then fell asleep, reassured.

The following morning, I didn't see her at breakfast. She hadn't left me any message. She had taken the car. So I went into her room; as usual, she had cleared out everything which had been there the previous day.

I was beginning to develop a taste for her sexual demonstrations. Doña Gloria had a very peculiar way of acting out her sexuality. When she did not feel she was sufficiently expressive, she corrected the movements of her body, her gestures, her general appearance. She made me her witness, asked me if her penance was beautiful. Sometimes I took the reins of her pleasures and made her take a rest to avoid carelessness and mistakes. One evening, I had suggested that she should take a shower to rinse off the sweat which covered her body with the wounds of penance.

She accepted. I ran the piping hot water over her fleshy, firm, robust body. And I ran a sponge down her legs, between her thighs, around her breasts as the water trickled over them. I remembered the two Venezuelans, Carlotta and Yolanda, who had taught me that in the shower.

The first contact of my hands on her body electrified her. Doña Gloria found the session exceptionally beneficial for her meditation. That was the evening when she returned from town after going to find out about the good works she had set in motion. She told me about the papers she was going to obtain for me so that I could stay in Spain, and I thanked her. But it was she who thanked me for I provided her with important services concerning her *Spiritual Exercises*. Doña Gloria had a proper sense of what was polite.

When she abandoned herself with me to these taxing yet also liberating games, she forgot them the next day, as if her memory had got rid of them during the night. For me, it was a sort of haven: and I no longer feared anything.

The three first weeks went by according to the programme which she had imposed upon herself. She walked round the house on her knees. She carried stones in her hands and stretched out her arms sideways to say her prayers. She asked me to chase her, and when I caught her I beat her backside with thongs. She lay crushed and humiliated on the cold ground and I had to give her my *carnal lance*. Then she stayed on her knees and sucked me frantically. Sometimes I was obliged to plead tiredness for she was never worn out. She prepared me a snack with sweetmeats and fruit, before going off to attend to her household duties.

The dinners which followed became flamboyant ceremonies. Doña Gloria forgot her mourning. She wore magnificent evening dresses – sometimes black, sometimes red. Her breasts floated behind the silk or the jersey, her hips falling freely; broad belts cut across her waist and made her exciting, ready to be devoured.

One evening, as I was about to sit down at the table, I heard her voice but didn't know where it was coming from. I sat down, then I felt something moving under the table. She moved towards my legs, parted them, unbuttoned my trousers and took out my lance. When I had given her my carnal essence, she withdrew and we were able to begin the meal. She said nothing. By way of recompense, she smiled at me constantly. This was her only form of language during the course of several evenings.

One of these so-called penitential evenings was entitled: humility. The dining-room was lit by candles which gave out a weak light. Doña Gloria told me that she was going to serve dinner as a servant and, each time she infringed the rules of proper formal service, I should correct her in whatever way I chose. So I took my place at the table, and saw her come out of the kitchen wearing a strange outfit. She was wearing a black apron which covered her belly and cunt, and a white collar which formed a circle on her chest. Underneath, she was completely naked. Her backside was also open to the air. The thongs were on a small round table not far from my chair. I began to eat. When I wanted a drink, she filled my glass. When I took some salt, she was disconsolate and apologized for the dishes not being sufficiently seasoned for my taste. She begged me to make her undergo a forfeit. She had caught me unawares. She approached me and offered me her fleshy, firm, swelling buttocks. She pushed her backside out even further and asked me to beat her. 'Again, again, again', she said, another ten times. I gave her a spanking then she thanked me that she had felt its warmth so keenly.

I wanted some wine. I pushed my glass in her direction and she picked up the carafe and moved towards my plate. The wine trickled slightly on to the napkin which I had placed on my knees. She noticed this, crouched down and licked the drop of wine off the serviette. I took out my lance which she took into her mouth, then licked it along its entire length, with minute attention to detail. She staunched her thirst little by little with the touch of her lips. I made her stop caressing me as I wanted to save myself for the rest of the ceremony.

60

She waited upon me until the end of the meal. She worked hard at it, but I found her a little too fussy and fidgety. I brought this to her attention. That seemed to please her. I saw her breasts thrusting past the sort of ruffle she was wearing. I drew her towards me, advising her not to make them thrust out so quickly and so surreptitiously. I then pinched their tips and pressed them between my fingers. 'Harder,' she urged me. Her pleasure mounted and I beat her backside again. She twisted and turned admirably and gave out roars of satisfaction. Then I caressed her pubis whilst she stood up straight. My hand brushed her nether lips and I could feel her becoming moist. She guided me. I caressed her under her buttocks and thrust my fingers deep into her cunt. Suddenly she picked up a little cucumber which was in the vegetable dish and handed it to me. I put it into her and beat time. When I felt her pleasure rising I ordered her to come and sit on me. I then told her that she was not displaying her pleasure fittingly. She hurriedly came over and bore down on my lance. I had been waiting for this moment for a long time. She turned her back to me and her body rose and fell; she moaned lasciviously whilst I pressed her breasts.

I made her speed up the rhythm. She did so and her buttocks enfolded me completely. She began to weaken. I brought this to her attention so that she would apologize. She literally melted with pleasure, throwing her head forward on to the table. I was still hard. I lifted her up and laid her against the table.

With all my strength, I pushed my lance into the depths of her cunt, which was frothing with pleasure. She cried out several times and I filled her to overflowing. For a little while I remained on top of her body as she caught her breath before plunging into a state of sublime wellbeing. She continued to guide me, facilitating the least little activities.

After this episode, she went up to her room, I was to join her in the darkness, completely naked and ready to climb into her bed. She was waiting for me, done up like a prostitute. She was wearing stockings held up by red silk garters, a lacy miniskirt and a corset which compressed her breasts and made them thrust upwards magnificently. I had to give my opinion on her outfit, which I did. Then I got on to the bed. She praised my body and its actions. That evening, she wished to attain all the pleasure which her body and her soul could give. She approached the bed and placed herself between my legs. She licked them and reached my lance which she brushed lightly. Next, Doña Gloria rubbed her breasts on my belly, then on my torso, before giving them to me to bite and suck. When she felt me big and swollen in her hand, she flung herself on to my lance and pumped away until the carnal essence – as she always called it – spattered out on to her face. That was her secret pleasure. Then she drew away and stood against the wall.

I had to inspect her body before penetrating it from behind, as she wished. Then I tied her up again and whipped her buttocks with thongs. I had to lick her all over. In a final intoxication of the senses, she wanted to sup once more at my spring whilst I thrust my tongue into the hollow of her cunt, smelling the rosewater which she was constantly exuding. That excited me. She made me give up the ghost and stretched herself all down my body, kissing my feet.

Those nights were hot with passion. My extreme youth made it easy for me to fulfil the task in the *Exercises* which Doña Gloria imposed on herself and on me. But what I feared most were the whippings she begged me to give her. I tried to wriggle out of these penances by indicating bodily positions to her, with a view to a higher level of pleasure. I played with her body and she did beautiful acrobatics with hers. But after six weeks she steeped herself in her mystical books again and, each night, urged me to chain her up in various ways. On one occasion, she wanted to stay like that all night, at the foot of her bed. Another time, when she was stretched out on a table and chained up, I had to give her various tokens so that her body could *expiate* all the pleasure and pain of her sins! Those were her words. And my *carnal lance* was the instrument of her ardent repentance.'

With those words, Reinaldo stopped and cast a long, panoramic look around him. I followed the arc described by his head and my gaze fell on a mournfully beautiful face. Dressed in black, the figure's silhouette stood out in profile among the tables like an elf. As she went past, nothing moved until she had found a place to sit down. The night-time faces had given her a discreet welcome: mouths which opened and murmured words which only she could understand, movement of the eyelid worthy of a masterstroke, hands whose fingers expressed themselves through cabbalistic signs, all the charms of a noble salutation reserved for a few initiates. And this beauty was a southern beauty. One of those who seemed to know her was Reinaldo. Interrupting the thread of his story for a moment, he had given her a surreptitious wave of recognition. This exchange had all the qualities of a lightning flash, as though their spirits had touched, transcending their bodies.

This interlude had made me lose track of where we

had got to. I took up the conversation and asked Reinaldo:

'What happened after such a sensual night?'

'But . . . didn't you see that magnificent entrance?' he retorted, seething with fire!

'I noticed the secret understanding between you, her and the others. How could I have missed such grace!'

'She's an artiste, chosen by the gods. A nocturnal mirage. She has an incomparable lyricism. An inexplicable charisma! That young woman holds secrets in her hands, but her hour is yet to come.'

Reinaldo's voice seemed to be coming out of a dream which had no key. Then he gave me a smile, and began to talk again, rapidly.

'Oh yes! but you know . . . you can be light-years away from certain people's lives and be brought closer to them only by some tiny detail, an oh-so-enthralling detail, sweeping away all the rest. That's the case with this young woman, with whom I had that *feeling* – a two-way, sensitive, rare, shared feeling. Her gift is the gift of words. She takes you from one point to another without your having a chance to escape. Her stories outdo mine by a long way, in terms of the fantastical! And you already know how talkative I can be. . . .'

'I have my faults too. I can even be indiscreet. . . .'

'No, I'm talking to you because I like you. So, let's get back to Doña Gloria.'

Scarcely had his tone of voice changed when I felt even closer to him.

'I had to find a solution. But it's all so far away. I'm telling you my life-story in a curious way. It's as if the different episodes, with their continuous conveyor-belt of images, were overlapping and interlacing. But each event follows the preceding one as though foreseen by an implacable logic. As I relate them to you now, they assert themselves upon me like evidence.'

Reinaldo took up the thread of his story.

'Doña Gloria was beginning to wear me out. I had to get away from her during the daytime. Her maid-servant didn't come back. I had a pressing need to work if I was going to continue my journey. One day, I went to Cadiz and met Doña Gloria's old servant. I told her what I had resolved to do. I refrained from referring to the relationship between Doña Gloria and myself. But I did tell her about the severe penances she was inflicting on herself. The old serving-woman raised her arms to heaven. I asked her when she was coming back to take up her job. She told me she had another four weeks' holiday.

As I walked round Cadiz with this old woman, I asked her if it was possible to get a job. She thought I might be able to be a waiter in an inn or do some market-trading. The idea of the inn appealed to me more. She said she would soon give me some news.

Doña Gloria began to appreciate my escapades less

and less. To lessen her mood-swings, I offered her my services during the mornings, and urged her to pray, then prepare herself for the evening's rites. I surpassed myself in giving her all the pleasure she demanded. I anticipated her desires but one day she wanted to whip me, so that I could participate in the expiation of her sins.

And at that point, I slipped away. She wept. Then I tried to calm her down by taking her by surprise in her bedroom in the early morning or in the middle of the night. These theatricals lasted for a month.

Prior to this, I had seen Doña Gloria's servant several times in Cadiz. She showed me a district of the town where I might find a job. I visited it one afternoon. It was quite a lively area where people sang and danced in the street. The women flaunted their charms and the men courted them with a great deal of humour. I wandered about among these twisting streets so that I would be able to get my bearings later on. Afterwards, I went back to Doña Gloria's house.

One September night, I decided to leave. I got all my things together and took the papers which related to me. The old serving-woman had returned, and she helped me to get away in the middle of the night. But I left Doña Gloria Villanueva Y de Montero a long letter of thanks, explaining the cause of my departure: I had to continue my journey.

I left in the middle of the night on a bicycle which the old woman had given me. A feeling of loneliness came over me on the starlit road. I knew the way very well and had arranged several return trips long before when going to Cadiz. On a piece of paper I had drawn a plan which would allow me to find the district which I had visited a few weeks before. I crossed San Fernando and reached Cadiz in the darkness.

It was about one o'clock in the morning when I at last found the district. It was particularly lively, which put me in a good mood even though I didn't know where I was going to spend the night. I had dismounted from my bicycle. I crossed many winding streets where young boys were still having fun with girls of their own age. I ventured forth. Cafés were still open and musicians were playing *alegrias* and sang to their own accompaniment when the songs were not taken up by the assembled throng. I dawdled in front of these cafés, these little inns where a real night life existed. That was what I was looking for. Suddenly, I felt free.

I continued along these streets, and crossed a passage where prostitutes were plying their trade. The lights from bar-rooms shone through windows and lit up stretches of walls as well as the faces of young, and no-so-young, women. Their dresses were brilliantly coloured, even in the darkness. Some of them cast glances at me and called to me. I continued on my way.

It was late and I was still trailing along when I heard the sound of voices a hundred yards or so away. I tried to see where it was coming from. I walked round many, many winding streets, and spotted a woman struggling with two boys who seemed young to me. Perhaps without realizing what I was doing, I dropped my bicycle and ran towards them as fast as I could. I too began to shout. I told them to let go of the woman. The woman hurled violent insults at them. I asked her if she was at all hurt. She assured me that she wasn't. I picked up her handbag. She stared at me and asked me what I was doing there at that time of night.

I told her part of my story, and also that I found myself without anywhere to stay and without a job. She looked at me as if I was mad and I started to laugh.

She exclaimed: 'Oh! Boys – they're always wanting *cornetas*. I'm not a streetwalker, you know!'

She asked me my name; then decided to give me shelter for the night. I thanked her wholeheartedly, and followed her home.

She was called Mariola. Her red hair had a touch of blonde in it. Her large green eyes were constantly blinking, and she mesmerized me with her gaze. She was slender and must have been about thirty. Mariola had a profession: she was a bolero singer and a flamenco dancer. But she preferred singing. She knew Latin America through the tours she had made of it with a big orchestra when she was a young girl. She told me all of this as soon as we arrived at her little house, at the edge of the lively district we had just left. I was utterly worn out. She made up a bed for me and immediately I fell sound asleep.

I heard someone humming a tune. It seemed to me that I was being cradled by angels.

The next morning was not like the others. When I opened my eyes, I saw Mariola walk past in a mauve dressing-gown, with gold embroidery on the shoulders. Her hair was thrown back, forming a mass of waves which shone in the light. She gave me a smile and a wink which I returned and I stretched myself out in bed.

When I think back to those mornings, to all those women, *dear comrade*, whom I met during my adolescence and afterwards, I realize to what extent they have determined the course of my life. They have served as my angels and my demons. And, also, enigmas and abysses. I always wanted to approach them, even when they burned with a fire which instantly made me burst into flame.

Mariola took my hand right from the first morning. After lunch she did some dancing and singing practice. We had got up rather late. She could only keep me on one condition, she said: I must not get in the way when she was entertaining boyfriends. I must lose myself in the little bedroom which she had placed at my disposal. She would try to get me a job in the bar where she sang. It wasn't a foregone conclusion, and she advised me to go there in person to meet the owner. She would have a word with him. If the first bar wouldn't take me on, she would introduce me to other people. I thanked her for her initiative and gave her a loving look. She noticed it and, lifting up my face, told me that I must change my eyes if I wanted to stay at her house, as in the end they might melt . . .

Mariola had a good sense of humour, and I liked her expressions. When her hair fell carelessly over her eyes, her face took on an expression of desire. She moved gracefully, but from time to time the fruit of her experience rose to the surface, shining through in the way her mind was always quick to make decisions.

So I took myself off to the Flamingo, the bar which stood in the area of Cadiz renowned for nightlife. It wasn't yet open to customers. I went into that long room where the air was moist. At the far end, there was a stage which was used for performances and, on the left, a bar with a metallic surround. Long bunches of drapery hung from the ceiling, forming a sort of cupola. On the ground there were large stones. You'd have thought you were in a cave.

I asked for the person whose name Mariola had given me. After a few minutes the owner arrived.

I told him that it was Mariola who had sent me to him. I told him that I was Venezuelan, that my papers were in order, that I was ready to do any sort of work. He took stock of me rapidly, asked my age just for form's sake, and told me to come back the next day around noon. I thanked him and went off through the town, before going back to Mariola's house.

When I got back to the house, Mariola was saying goodbye to a man who was just about to leave. He wore a tight suit and a black hat. He looked like an undertaker's man. That image froze my blood. Mariola asked me how I'd got on.

When night fell, she got ready and I accompanied her to the Flamingo. That evening, she had to go and dance in another bar. She showed me the streets I must take to get there. The place was called the Tonadilla.

The street was lively and noisy. People were starting to go into the bar, Whilst I was still chatting with Mariola, men greeted her courteously. I left Mariola and went off towards the centre of Cadiz.

I came back two hours later. I caught sight of her: she was singing boleros. She moved in time to the music, and as she swayed her hips the line of her breasts began to tremble. Her scalloped bodice revealed her gleaming, nacreous flesh, bespattered with patches of red light. This sight electrified me. Mariola shone brilliantly when she sang, living the words completely. But I could not stay long in the half-open doorway, because people were coming in. I went back to the house, to wait until it was time for me to go back and fetch Mariola.

It was getting on for midnight when I walked back down to the Tonadilla.

Mariola was dancing to the tune of a bolero – what they call a fandango in Spain today. She was exciting everyone in the room. Her lasciviousness invoked desire, the intoxication of the senses. All faces were turned towards her. She gave me a strange feeling: all of a sudden, I wanted to drag her away from her public and make love to her.

That night gave off electricity, a magnetic field which reminded me of the fiestas in my native Venezuela. Bold, unrestrained dances like the bamba, the bambuco or the zamacueca. Mariola danced her boleros in time to the rhythm of the castanets, guitar chords and throbbing drum-rolls. She turned round, lifted first one leg then the other, stole away, drew close once more, and once again escaped from the audience which surrounded her. She danced like those Cuban negresses, maddened by the rhythm of the rumba. And in fact, after her recital and her show, she was asked to perform some Latin-American dances. And, at that moment, her face was radiant with a thousand burning fires, and her body was a tornado.

When it was all over, a man came to see her. He spoke to her in a low voice, standing close to the exit. She stood opposite him, haughty and majestic, listening as one might listen to a prayer. We left together. Once we were out of the district, Mariola took my arm. I paid her compliments, assuring her that she danced like the best dancers in Latin America. She smiled at me and I plucked up the courage to tell her that she was very beautiful. She pressed herself against me. Her body, the way her hips swayed, and her soft, mango-sweet flesh, sent shivers running through me. I stopped talking. She was the

73

one who spoke, telling me the story of her love of dancing.

She invited me to join her in her room, where she had kept the posters advertising performances on her famous tours. She showed me photos of her which had been published in magazines, and her wardrobe, which had quite a story to tell. In a corner of her bedroom, covered with bronze and mauve-coloured hangings, stood an old phonograph. She began to dance after getting changed behind a screen. Then she sang along to the voice coming out of the machine:

> I'd say the love of men
> Is like the climate of Madrid.
> One day the heat is torrid
> Then it's freezing cold again.
> My lass, men's vows of trust
> Are like ironmonger's tins:
> As shiny as new pins
> And three day's later, full of rust.

She laughed heartily at this song which she had performed when she was on tour. Then she took my hand and executed a difficult dance-step. I followed her, clumsily. Her eyes were shining, her hair straggled out of place and her scanty dress revealed the ivory colour of her breasts. We bumped into each other from time to time, and touched. I could no longer control myself. I slid my hands around her waist and made her twirl round. She continued:

Upon your wedding day
Listen, and you will hear
The organ's music say:
'You'll repent of this, my dear.

When the music stopped, her face fell a little.

'Now, I'm too old,' she said. 'Only the old gentle-men run after me – the young ones only want *cornetas*. Look where I've ended up. I sing, I dance, I go back home and bed down. Sometimes one or two men come and visit me and I give them a little fire, a little desire or *something else*. It's for that reason, Reinaldo, that you must go away when I ask you to. What's more, I don't know if I'm going to stay in Cadiz much longer. And what about you: do you desire me? Or am I too old. . . .'

I interrupted her. I told her that this evening she had been more beautiful than a young girl in the flower of youth. Neither her body nor her face had been spoiled by the passing of years. I babbled out a few more words, then ran into my bedroom. I couldn't contain myself any longer, and I was ashamed of desir-ing her.

Mariola was sending me into a paroxysmal state. My nerves were at fever-pitch; I was excited by the idea that I might caress the tiniest folds of her skin, embrace those mother-of-pearl domes, slide down the receding line of her legs and suffocate myself with pleasure by sucking her fur-trimmed lips.

All at once, a bittersweet music spread around me.

75

It was like fabrics rustling, jewels tinkling in a box, fine rain on a corrugated-iron roof, the ebb and flow of the sea. I had lain down on the floor of my bedroom.

I felt a cool, smooth gel spreading out, little by little, over my body. The scent of musk. Silken threads brushed my face, my neck, my torso. A stranger's skin was skimming over this surface which had been rendered painful by the contraction of my nerves, the violence of desire.

Stroking, breathing, whispering, all came to me as an echo. Delicate, deliberate pinches placed on different parts of my belly. I closed my arms on this magical presence, this wild force. I fell like a waterfall and flowed into the bed of a river in flood. Lianas interwove between my thighs and suddenly I felt the middle of my body breathed in, suckled. My head rolled between two soft, spongy rocks where the rapid rhythm of a heart was beating. My tongue tasted the juice which flowed from this starfish. It contracted, the more I teased it. It used its suckers like a peacock's feathers before closing them delicately around my ripe mango.

Anyone would have thought first one flower's petals, then petals in their thousands, were coming together in a hybrid dance like that of the *folia tulia*[1], along that wild, tropical stem. The rumbling grew louder

---

[1] A Portuguese dance which originated in carnival, and which is therefore a fertility dance. Known specifically for it gestures and postures.

and we rushed down, clinging to each other, through confused, limitless space. Nothing stopped us. The flower unfolded once again, and the fruit ripened a second time as it felt the contact of her mouth. Inhuman cries rose to a crescendo. Then, slowly, the waves ebbed away like caresses on the sand.

It was infinite ecstasy.

Mariola.'

'Day by day the time passed in Cadiz. I had started work at the Flamingo. The nights were hellish. I worked more than twelve hours a day and, in the evening, I waited for Mariola to finish her performing so that we could go home together. During my free time, I continued to improve my knowledge of French and English. When tourists visited the bars I frequented, I talked to them. From time to time I acted as their guide, which gave me a little pocket-money. Once, I was tempted to go to Madrid. For Mariola often spoke to me about that town where she had been queen of the night. But I still needed to stay with her. She inspired a violent passion in me.

Mariola's night-life was a sarabande. I was her plaything, the servant of her whims, the arbiter of her sordid transactions. My presence at her side was not always a tranquil one. I had to put up with being teased by the men who followed her about in the taverns.

Sometimes I was called *el niño*, sometimes Mariola's

mango. These jests related to the fact that she was my protector.

This state of affairs disappeared as the months went by.

What hurt me most of all, *dear comrade*, was seeing this woman, this goddess of beauty and sensual pleasure, yielding to certain men's deviations. Mariola was an artiste who had gained a tremendous reputation in the capital. All Madrid used to come and see her dance and sing. And then, one day, a wealthy and famous man wanted her all to himself. When she gave in to him, she stopped performing. It was a sacrifice for her, because she was only twenty-two at the time. She had made a name for herself in less than five years. And she never regained that peak of fame. Many years later, when the man who had taken her away from her public and her art suddenly disappeared, she was left abandoned and penniless. She had to leave the town and travel all over Spain, from tavern to tavern, encountering on her journey all the trials and tribulations of an itinerant life. Then she came and settled in Cadiz, where there could be no one left who remembered what she had been in her youth.

I learned to know Mariola and she taught me a lot. My character formed and my desires became many and varied. She guided them and restrained them simultaneously. I was growing and needed new horizons. As for Mariola, she lived as she always did, and had no goal in mind. Perhaps she had become resigned to it? Perhaps she didn't even realize she was doing it?

But the memories I kept of her were very intense. Especially my memories of evenings in the taverns. One night I had witnessed one of the strangest scenes of my life.

The Tonadilla was full to bursting that evening, a season before I left Cadiz. *Majos* and *majas*, those boys and girls dressed in the gaudiest colours, were strutting up and down nonchalantly at the far end of the cabaret room.

The first seats were taken immediately and some people were even sitting on the ground to follow the new show which Mariola was putting on with her dancers. Showbills had been posted up in the town, proclaiming the fact that Cuban musicians would accompany the great bolero singer.

I then watched the audience: their faces were tense and screwed up, their gazes all converging on a single point. They all wore an expression of supreme expectancy. The men's foreheads were furrowed in expressions worthy of being featured in character studies. Their breathing exuded a strange music. Their eyes were popping out of their sockets. And their mouths were twisted with desire.

The first guitar-chords rang out. Men, black and proud, walked on from either side of the stage as the curtains opened. The lights went down and the drums set the rhythm. The room fell silent. Mariola looked vibrant right from the first bars of the song. She was wearing a sort of dress with red and gold embroidered fringes which snaked like lianas across her thighs and legs. The upper part of the dress lay across her breasts in the shape of a spindle, revealing her ivory flesh, sparkling with life. A black leather belt cut across her waist and showed off the roundness of her hips.

Mariola – this woman whom people had come to see from all over the region – was a woman desired, lusted after; a woman who aroused every kind of madness! Influential people had reserved tables. Fanatical suitors came back time and time again to see her. They all came there to experience a sensation of lasciviousness which could not be found anywhere else.

Mariola began a languid song, describing concentric circles with her arms and surprising arabesques with her hands. You'd have thought she was a Hindu goddess. But her body expressed the many peculiarities of a limitless dance. The timbre of her voice changed from the earthy raucousness of the Cuban jungle, to an Andalusian lament, to the sourish lightness of an old Spanish song – the tirana. She moved her legs backwards and forwards rapidly, baring them in an orgy of stage-lights. The audience shouted with joy. Her dance became faster and faster. You'd have thought she was a burning torch, set aflame by the rhythm. Her face was radiant, reflecting the desire of those who were watching. Her earrings jingled, her fiery hair cut jerkily through the air, then fell back down over her breasts and shoulders. For a moment, her gaze was fixed on the horizon, and then lingered on the front row. She moved towards the VIPs and turned round suddenly and passionately, and with her back to them she ran her hands over her body, from her twin water-melons to the base of her fleshy, tapering thighs. Mariola gave full rein to her wild, sensual gestures. The whole room was soon in an uproar.

For her finale, she began an old, slow rumba. The musicians strummed the strings of their guitars lasciviously whilst a percussionist dictated the rhythm, which was getting faster, little by little. At that moment, some spectators stood up to dance as they watched Mariola. Then shouts rang out as she began to sing:

> A half-caste woman's killed me
> Won't anyone arrest her?
> Which of us will stay alive
> If murderers go free?
> Like bread, these half-caste women fine
> Must be eaten warm,
> If you let them get too cold
> The devil himself won't dine.

Suddenly, the spectators felt that, at this moment in the song, they could possess Mariola. And Mariola danced whilst the musicians improvised between each verse. They walked to the front of the stage and made Mariola disappear behind them, leaving the first row stretching their hands out into emptiness. Then she came back after a few catlike steps and continued:

No half-caste woman's lovelier
More rascally or hotter
And nor compared to Rose's rump
Could any arse be softer.

She rippled her body sensually at the word 'arse' and interlaced her fingers over her cunt at 'Rose', then slid her hands over her hips. This marked her deification in the cabaret-room.

Behind me, I felt a strange presence. There was quite a tall man wearing a dark hat and suit. He jostled a few people before rushing out. It seemed to me that I had seen him before. But where?

The show ended a few minutes later. And Mariola received flowers amid thunderous applause. She was as divine as ever. I was to meet up with her at the stage-door. I dawdled in the hall for a while, then walked up and down the street, watching the motley, multi-coloured fauna as they came out.

When I went round to the back door, the man I had seen before in the hall was there. The musicians began to come out and waited for Mariola. She arrived, laughing lustily. The musicians congratulated her noisily whilst the man stood not far away from them. Mariola noticed that he was there. She moved away from the circle (of musicians) and walked towards him. He greeted her with a kiss on the hand. Now I recognized him. He was the one who had already waited for her several times when she finished her evening circuit in Cadiz. I couldn't put an age on him. But his hair was quite long. His profile stood out against everyone else's. He seemed to belong to a different era.

I was still the same distance away when Mariola cast a glance in my direction. She exchanged a few words with the man and came to meet me.

She then told me to go home ahead of her, to stay in my room and not make a sound. I would find a note on my bedside table which would tell me what to do tonight. She would be coming back very soon. She squeezed my hand then kissed me on the forehead. And I left, glancing one last time at this man who waited for her in the darkness.

It's that particular night, that scene, of mingled pain and pleasure, *dear comrade*, to which I was referring. It concerned Mariola. I then went back to the house and read the few sentences she had left me on a piece of paper. I was to go along a corridor which ran behind her bedroom, then into a room which served as a lumber-store. On the wall hung an old painting. On removing it, I would find a crack in the wall which would allow me to see and hear what might happen in her bedroom. There was also a hanging thread which linked the two rooms. If I saw it disappear, I was to come into her room immediately. But on no account was I to watch through this opening.

I settled myself down there and waited for something to happen.

I heard footsteps. Mariola was not alone. The drawing-room was behind the corridor I had used. She raised her voice and I realized that she was giving orders. He was to wait for her. She went into her bedroom. I strained my ears so that I would hear the tiniest sound. There were a few minutes of silence, and she called out. The footsteps – long strides – set off in the direction of her bedroom. A dull, heavy sound rang out as something hit the ground. What could be happening? I came closer to the wall and listened intently.

Some more dull sounds, heavy and confused, rang out behind the partition wall. Then I noticed a sort of low, hoarse moan. A thick, oily, throaty sound. It wasn't Mariola. Then I heard her voice: 'Come on slowly.' That was all. But I was intrigued and moved slowly towards the crack.

Mariola was perched on high heels, her thighs clad in black stockings and her hands on her hips. She was wearing lace panties, her leather belt, and two circles of copper confined her breasts. Her lips seemed outrageously painted. Her face wore an expression of madness.

On the ground a man was watching her, on all fours, and was moving towards her. It was indeed the one who had been waiting for her. I saw his long shock of hair hanging down behind his bare neck. He seemed to be pleading with her. She turned round and he threw himself at her feet. She repulsed him violently and moved away from his axis. She began to laugh. And I heard this man's frail voice. A voice which was indefinable because it seemed to emanate from a young girl's body. He then said very weakly, in a shrill register: 'I want to know that through you! Give me that chance.' Mariola kicked her heel into his hands. He leapt up, took off her shoe and began to lick her feet with devotion. I saw Mariola resist when he began to move upwards towards her leg. She stopped him in his tracks and said: 'This is your final humiliation! She pushed him off again and he sprawled in the middle of the room, half-naked. Suddenly, this man covered his face with his hands and wept. Mariola walked round him and crouched down by his side, taking his head in her arms, drawing it to the hollow between her nacreous, copper-covered domes. She cradled him for a moment. He was calmed.

I turned away from this sight. There was silence. An overwhelming silence. What was Mariola to this strange man? What did he want from her that he could not find elsewhere?

I listened to the murmuring of his faint, feeble breathing on the other side of the wall. The man was fretting like a child. He lay there, trying to get Mariola to console him. She had caressed his pale face. She had accepted this ceremony with its psychological meanderings, a ceremony to which they alone held the keys.

The sound began again. I saw Mariola turn him over and slowly remove his trousers, then his underpants. He let her do it, completely dazed. He stretched out his hands to caress her between her legs and she gave him a slap. She made him put his hands behind his back and began to awaken his prick. This woman – I can assure you – was a real smooth operator. And this man who was experiencing the effects of Mariola's violent, seismic tremors remained inert, feeling nothing but pain.

Mariola's face grew drawn and she saw that this hybrid being was weeping. She moved away from him, shouting: 'Nothing! You carry a curse, and you'll always carry it!' She was panting and he dissolved into tears, covering his face. Mariola pushed back her hair. The prick had remained lifeless. And yet Mariola was an expert in erotic rites.

She drew herself up straight and disappeared whilst the man was still on the ground. Then in a flash, the man stood up. His face was suddenly transformed. Mariola appeared once again, bringing with her a basket whose contents I could not see. She turned round and moved over to a little round table.

The tall figure trembled. Fascinated by the sight, Mariola settled herself in the big armchair which she had in her bedroom. I had a sideways view of her. The man took little steps towards her. But she ordered him to get down on all fours. He followed her orders.

Mariola was wiggling about in her chair, making an indefinable sound. She seemed to be pushing something into herself. Then she stood up. Suddenly the man exulted, came towards her on all fours and walked round the armchair, sticking out his tongue like a devil. I didn't know what could possibly account for his being in such a state. Then he came to a halt opposite her and said: 'Is it true it's green, is it really green and does it belong to you?' Mariola nodded to him and asked him to approach her slowly.

He started to have a sort of epileptic fit. Mariola threw her head back and began to laugh like a mad-woman. I looked at what was sticking out from between her thighs. A blunt, rounded object pointed towards the man who was now a few centimetres away. She took hold of his head and brought it towards the precious object.

I then heard dry, smacking, sucking noises. The scene, which Mariola was directing, plunged me into a state of complete bewilderment. The man was taking his pleasure between her thighs with a strange instrument between him and her.

Then the man collapsed, revealing the outline of his thighs and two scraggy hemispheres. This night had awakened another facet of love in Mariola, a facet which only a few fetishists know. She too was trembling. And, in an ultimate act of violence, she crouched down opposite him and pushed that object up his backside.

This sight disturbed me and I fled. When I got back to my room, I could hear shouts, childish bawling. Then a voice, and laughter: Mariola's voice and Mariola's laughter.

Later on that night, I heard footsteps going towards the door to the street. Then I felt someone was coming in the direction of my room. I pretended to be asleep. It was Mariola. She called to me but I did not reply.'

'When I awoke the next morning, I felt nauseous. I went into the kitchen to make some coffee. Mariola wasn't there. I looked for her in the living-room, then knocked on her door. No one replied. No doubt she had gone out. I went back into the kitchen. I poured myself a coffee. Suddenly, my eyes lighted on the basket of fruit and vegetables which stood on the dresser. My gaze dwelt for some time on something green and long. At that moment I understood all of what had happened the previous night between Mariola and that strange being. Immediately I left the kitchen, vomiting uncontrollably.

I forced myself to think about something else and I went for a swim. When I got back to the house, Mariola still wasn't there. I absorbed myself in my books and thought of the photo which was so dear to me. It gave me back my courage and I imagined a thousand things, a thousand adventures.

Summer was drawing to a close and I spent another

year at Mariola's house, but I kept my distance from her, then made preparations for my departure. Since leaving Venezuela, I had been writing to a friend of my father's and he sent me details for my journey.

The following summer, I conceived a plan to go to Bilbao with friends, then to England. I didn't know how to tell Mariola about it.

One Saturday morning, when she was at the market, I left her a message, did my packing and got my things together. I didn't tell her that I wasn't coming back.

I met up with my friends and we took a bus to Bilbao, but stayed there only a short while, before leaving to continue our journey to London.

During the journey we played the fool. And sometimes we took with us girls we had met in the towns we went through. One of these was English – a blonde with reddish highlights, whose name was Glenda.

This episode only left me with a fleeting memory compared with the earlier ones, and even those ended up becoming blurred.

I read in a book that: *adventure does not exist. It is in the mind of the person who pursues it, and, as soon as he can touch it with his fingers, it vanishes, only to reappear much further away, in another shape and form . . .'*

Reinaldo stopped suddenly, then looked around him. Was he looking for the southern beauty? A fleshy redhead had taken her place.

Reinaldo turned to me.

'It's strange, the way memories return just when you're not expecting them to! For example, I can remember a girl I was in love with and who wanted to make a life with me, but she couldn't put up with my friends. We split up. But where had we got to?'

'After your time with Mariola. Did you ever see her again?' I asked him.

'No. I was tempted to go back and look for her in Cadiz, because I was going through a bad patch. But I never take a backward step.'

'When night was falling, I sometimes used to see Mariola's image reflected in my mind.

But Glenda was beginning to mean something to me.

It was in the mountains, in a sort of no-man's-land between Spain and France, that I first set out to get to know her body better. And the fruits which she had to offer me, although they were not yet ripe, were nevertheless appetizing.'

'So in the end you went to England with Glenda?' I asked Reinaldo, who was lost in his memories.

'Yes, whilst we were together, she introduced me to her mother's cousin, who had married an old peer. He was one of a kind! That's a digression which I shall tell you about. But when I was in London – after a period of relative calm – I had to take a decision. I was tempted to follow Glenda, but it was impossible because I was running out of cash.'

'What did you do?'

'First of all, I went to the immigration office. After

93

that, I had to do anything I could to get by. That's when the following events happened to me.'

'When I first entered the house of Lord Ian Worth-wilde and his wife Veronica, an Indian manservant was working for them. He seemed tired out by the weight of his years. Lord Ian had brought him back from India with him. Although he'd been in the house for around twenty years, Lord Ian's wife was only just getting used to him. What's more, Veronica was much younger than her husband and found it difficult to put up with the valet's fads and fancies, however devoted he might be to his master.

Two weeks later, to my surprise, it was Glenda who opened the door and let me in. The manservant had retired. Veronica seemed both delighted and embarrassed at the same time. I told Glenda about my problems and I asked her if she could tell her cousin about them. I had to stay in London a while longer, and I needed a job and a roof over my head; Glenda thought it was an excellent idea. She arranged a meeting, at teatime, with Lord Ian.

Veronica greeted me with a broad smile. She was wearing a long white dress with an embroidered bodice; the dress fluttered about as she moved. She sparkled, and was never lost for a witty remark. She couldn't have been more than thirty-five. Lord Ian had stayed locked away in his library, where she had taken him his tea rather sulkily.

When I explained to her why I needed to remain

in London, she immediately understood what I was getting at. So I voiced my request. Veronica took the idea very well. But she still had to convince Lord Ian to take me into their service. I remained lost in thought for a moment. Then she began to speak and said to me: 'I've wanted to learn Spanish for a long time.' It was my big chance . . . I said I thought it was an excellent idea. She told us about her many travels and the love she had for Spanish folklore, costumes and music.

Then she arranged to meet me again the following day. Glenda was hopeful. That evening, she showed me round several parts of London: Soho, Piccadilly and Chelsea. Veronica Worthwilde lived in Sloane Square, not far from a park, behind King's Road. I wanted to go back to Soho, and Glenda had said she would take me there. In fact, a Venezuelan friend of mine had given me some information about my mother: before returning to France, she had taught French in London in this well-known district. I had only a vague address, but I hoped that my research would bear fruit.

The following morning, Glenda went with me to Soho. We walked down Wardour Street. I looked round for the approximate location of the address where there was supposed to be a French language institute. An old lady, who was standing on her balcony, called down to us. Glenda told her that we were looking for a French institute. The old lady replied that there hadn't been one around there for ages. I then thought of other possible leads in my search but I decided not to tell Glenda about them.

It was time for my meeting with Veronica. She opened the door to us with a smile. She was wearing a royal blue suit with a rare air of distinction. Her legs were superb.

I looked closely at her face. She had well-defined cheekbones, as fine as those of an eighteenth-century figurine, giving her a pert, childish look. Her deep-blue, almond-shaped eyes emphasized the deep intelligence of her gaze. Since the day before, everything about her had changed. I found this woman entirely engrossing. She greeted me cheerily: 'Now you're a part of this household!' I breathed a sigh of relief and gazed deeply into her eyes. I smiled at her and thanked her passionately.

She showed me my room and gave me a tour of the house and garden – she was a passionate gardener.

At seven-thirty precisely, Lord Ian left the library and came into the drawing room, where Glenda and I were sitting whilst Veronica prepared dinner. We got to know each other a little better, and he welcomed me to his house.

He was a travel-worn man of about fifty. His temperament was taciturn and reserved. He kept asking his wife Veronica if she had had a good day. Lord Ian asked me a few questions about where I came from. At the end of this charming dinner, he told me that his wife would instruct me the following day in the running of the house. Then he went and shut himself in the library again, and for a moment Veronica's face fell. The evening was cut short, as Glenda was leaving London the following morning.

When I lay down on my bed, I took out the photo of my mother. I was still thinking about the disappointment I'd had when I went to Soho. But I wasn't going to admit defeat . . .

Glenda left at around eight o'clock. Veronica and I accompanied her. On the way back, the stopped off in a bookshop. She got some Spanish textbooks and an English grammar. She asked me to explain about my lessons. She was happy and gave me a book. I was beginning to find it disturbing, having her by my side.

Veronica showed me what had to be done in that great house. Each day, I must bring the newspapers to Lord Ian and prepare afternoon tea for four p.m. precisely. She explained all the household chores, etc. But on no account must I go into her husband's library. He took care of it himself. Whenever I wanted to let him know that I was there, all I needed to do was pull on a cord which hung in the drawing-room and a little bell would alert him. As for lesson times, they still had to be sorted out.

My first days in the Worthwildes' house passed uneventfully. I spent my free time looking round London. I was at their service whenever they wished. And they complimented me on the way I carried out my duties and the dishes I cooked for them. Sometimes, Veronica asked me to go shopping with her. She showed me the shops in Kensington and the market in Portobello Road. When we were alone, she no longer wore the same expression as when she was with her husband. She had long conversations with me.

At the beginning of the second week, events took another turn. Lord Ian did not come into the dining-room for dinner. Veronica prepared a tray for him and took it into the library, where he shut himself away practically all day long. Veronica then told me he was working on an important project. So I began the evening alone with her. I felt awkward and embarrassed.

We had begun our Spanish lessons, too, settling to our studies. Veronica seemed delighted with this new-born complicity.

Her attic studio, where she painted watercolours, became our meeting-place. There was little furniture in the room: a large armchair, two chairs and a sort of settee. This first session threw my mind into confusion. Veronica's formidable presence, alone with me, awakened my senses. Until then, I had had no complaints about women! And so I was starting off in life with this irreplaceable knowledge.

Just as I had dreamed she would, Veronica asked me to sit down beside her, and opened a book. Her body exuded a perfume of sweet violets and lemons. Her dress brushed against my leg, causing a sensation like a myriad bee-stings to run up it. Her movements buzzed in my ears. Her melodious voice rose and fell through the whole range of sweet, low tones which made her so charming. She read a few poems in English and endeavoured to translate them into Spanish. And in this way I learned about the meaning which words could hide.

But Veronica could not hide the excitement which she felt when she was close to me. She asked me how certain words should be pronounced, and rolled her tongue around to form the exact sounds. I watched her smiling face. I could not hide the desire which she aroused in me. I began to smile at her and engaged her in conversation. I talked about her husband, Lord Ian. That made her give a long sigh. I apologized.

Lord Ian was a man who had made an overnight decision to live in almost complete self-sufficiency. Five years ago, after resigning from office, he had broken off relations with his family. And the taste for life had ebbed away from him. He had persuaded Veronica to stop giving dancing-lessons. She had been a real star in the world of dance. I then understood why she had done her utmost to keep me in her house.

She asked me nonchalantly if I understood the situation. I stared deep into her eyes and shook my head. She then resumed her study of the text which we were translating, placing her hand suddenly on my knee. I shall always remember that poem: 'What is your innocence, what is your guilt? All are naked, none is safe.' And I translated it approximately for her: 'Cual es nuestra inocencia, y cual nuestra culpa? Somos desnudos, y en inseguridad.' She found that very musical, and said to me with a hint of malice in her eyes: 'But you're quite safe here, aren't you?'

Then her hand stroked my thigh, and she placed the other on my arm. When Veronica's skin brushed my arm she excited me instantly. She was visibly waiting for an answer, and I didn't know what to say to her. Mechanically, I repeated the phrases which we had translated and, clumsily as I shifted position on my chair, I entwined my leg with hers. I fell against her and we both toppled over, landing on the carpet, with a warm, dull sound. I was lying on top of her, with my head buried in her bosom. I could feel her supple, pointed little breasts. We were more frightened than hurt. She laughed and rolled over, ending up on top of me. When I slid my hand over her slender buttocks, stretched taut by the movement, her face lit up. And I waited. Suddenly, a bell jangled. Veronica stood up quickly. It was coming from the drawing-room. Lord Ian had rung for service.

She ran downstairs. Then, a few minutes later, she called up to tell me that I could carry on with my duties. She would attend to her husband, she told me. I could come out, and that was what I wanted to do.

Veronica had enflamed my senses in a lightning-flash. I saw myself rolling on to the floor of her studio with her, then everything stopped short. I decided to go to Soho again, to cast new light on the problem of the address.

In Soho, I met some prostitutes soliciting not far from the street I'd gone to with Glenda. I gained a little more information than I had done the first time. I found out that there had indeed been a French mission round here. I was given the name of an old woman: she had been around in those days. I went to see her. Then, on a final impulse, I showed her the photo I had. She recognized the face. She then told me that this woman had gone back to Paris. Now I was sure that she was living in that city. I forgot about everything else.

When I got back to Sloane Square, it was already seven o'clock. There wasn't a sound to be heard in the house. Veronica wasn't in the drawing-room. There was only one place she could be, and that was the library. But the library was out of bounds to me.

I went off to get the dinner ready. At seven-thirty p.m. the house was still wreathed in silence. So I decided to go for a stroll in the garden. As I walked round the outside of the house, I noticed a light coming out of one of the rooms. It must be Lord Ian's library. I walked across a flowerbed and went towards the source of the light. Although the curtains were closed, there was a slight gap which allowed me to see inside.

Lord Ian was sitting behind a large table and I saw Veronica handing him a drink. At first sight, I hadn't noticed how she was dressed. She was wearing a bright coloured Indian sari which clung to her body, showing its curves off admirably. Suddenly, whilst Lord Ian moved his hand around her head, she began to dance. Her hands spun round in the air, her fingers executed a precise set of movements and described languid poses on either side of her face. She turned her knees out sideways, bending her legs, and flexed her body sinuously.

This surprised me. Lord Ian was in raptures. His face contorted itself into a grotesque expression as Veronica kept up her rhythm. After a quarter of an hour, she came towards her husband and slapped him violently. He began to laugh, throwing his head backwards. I saw her undressing in a corner of the library. At that moment, I returned to the kitchen.

Veronica came to find me so that we could go in to dinner. Her face betrayed not a trace of what had happened. She asked me if I had had a good afternoon and apologized for not being able to go through with the lesson.

After dinner, I went up quickly to my bedroom. I wanted to finish a French book. Veronica was surprised to see me disappear so quickly.

I worked out how long I would have to stay in London before leaving for Paris. This thought never left me. Whilst I waited, I must send a letter to my Venezuelan friend, then I would do some reading. But I just couldn't concentrate. I was obsessed by the sight which I had had of Veronica that afternoon.

Just as I was trying to get to sleep, I heard footsteps. They were coming towards my door. Then the door was open. Veronica murmured my name and came into the room; she called me again. I remained silent.

I held my breath. Then she sat on the bed and leant

over my face. She stroked my hair with her hand. Suddenly her hand slid under the sheet which covered me. I turned on to my back, and her hand withdrew. I gave no sign that I was awake. Then the hand came back and slid the length of my thighs. She gave a sigh and climbed into the bed. She brushed me with the tips of her breasts, which were covered with a flimsy silk. She rolled over my body and lowered herself between my legs, which I had parted.

She rolled her breasts over my prick with a steady motion. I felt myself trembling. She called to me once more. I let her continue. The sea-swell was beginning to roar. Then I grabbed hold of her head and pushed it down towards my belly. She gave out a stifled sound. And she placed her two hands round my waist. I put one leg in between her long, firm thighs and rubbed her mossy triangle. She melted on to my prick and pressed her breasts all around it. She rubbed it rhythmically. Then she drew her tongue around the end, twisted it around and closed her lips smoothly upon me. She ravaged me for at least half an hour.

She left me as stiff as a ship's mast. Whilst I was drawing away to turn her over, she wanted to get up. She lay on the edge of the bed and invited me to take her like that. Her muscular buttocks contracted as I pressed myself against her. I kneaded her breasts and she moaned like someone singing sentimental songs. When she spread her legs, I began to penetrate her from behind, burying myself in the depths of her with one, great thrust of my pelvis. She stuck her backside out further so as to make it easier for me to enter her. Then she clenched her thighs and held me there by gripping my buttocks with her hands. This gave me an enormous thrill, as she herself accentuated every second thrust, then every third, then I lost count. She burned me, tore me apart as she moved frenetically. She changed rhythm and crossed her thighs as hard as she could. She held me and I thrust deep inside her; her head shook. I was not in a very secure position, but I took one of her breasts and rubbed it. She began to cry out with pleasure and, imitating the way she had accentuated first each sixth and then each third thrust, I shot out my liquid into her, in a single draught. She stifled the sound of her orgasm by biting her fingers.

She pulled away from me, and I took her in my arms and drew her back in to the bed. She had begun to weep and was caressing my face. I licked away the tears which flowed down her cheeks and caught them as they ran down the length of her long, quivering neck. She calmed down and eventually began to smile again. She had longed so much for this moment. And she told me of those painful moments she had spent with her husband over the past years. I listened to her without saying a word, caressing her belly, thighs and breasts. Veronica was in the prime of life.

I then confessed to her that she had filled me with desire from our very first meeting. She wanted to talk and I put my hand on her lips. I slid down the length of her body, clinging close to the folds of her hips which I bit into like a juicy fruit. She stretched out her arms and took hold of my head. I slid down her belly and reached her liquid, fragrant island. I ventured forth like a vagabond on a deserted beach. I traced lines on the hot sand, then infinite circles. The water advanced little by little, forming vague shapes. Then I began to go in deeper, towards the sea. The waves slapped against my face then I lost my balance and fell over. I let myself be carried by the gentle, continuous movement of the deep ebb and flow of the rising tide. I felt a starfish rub itself against me. The tide around the central part of me grew, and I flowed back into the depths of a mass of seaweed. Borne away by the current, I found myself back on the beach. I held on tight, digging my fingers into the sand.

Veronica was that rough sea, that starfish. And she and I alike had been carried away by that tornado which had raged forth upon our burning bodies.

Veronica never ever mentioned that night. Nor did she make any further allusion to Lord Ian's eccentric tastes. But on several occasions she gave me a demonstration of her talents as a dancer and of her womanly nature, as fiery and burning as Africa. She was a born actress. And it was during our Spanish lessons, in the afternoons, that our secret meetings took place.

The pace of these lessons varied, according to the progress which Veronica made, or delays in study. I was the teacher and she asked me to exercise my authority. In addition, she added her own stamp to the proceedings, and this consisted of being a docile, childlike pupil. Childlike, because she dressed up in a little short skirt, which looked like a tutu, and a tight blouse which clung close to her breasts. In her hair, she wore two ribbons which fluttered about when she moved.

She came and sat down next to me, and we opened our books. She had to be scolded for each mistake she made. To facilitate this, on the table she had placed a wooden ruler about eighteen inches long, and I was to use it if she persisted in her clumsiness. She delighted in this. One day, she ordered me to deal with her severely. Seeing me hesitate, she put the ruler into my hands. She turned round and presented me with her buttocks, which formed taut swelling mounds. So I gave her a dozen or so light strokes with the ruler, as she asked me. She mimicked surprise and gave out little cries at the imaginary pain. She wasn't wearing any knickers.

Next, I made her sit down again next to me and continued the grammar and translation exercises. She got everything mixed up. I put on a horror-stricken look; I was playing her game. Suddenly, she got up from her chair and went to the foot of the bed. She bent over the end and laid her head against the mattress. I followed her, with the ruler in my hand. I lifted up her little skirt whilst, little by little, she spread her legs. And, after a few light strokes of the ruler, she swayed from right to left. In fact, she

106

wanted me to slide this long wooden stem in between her two tapering domes, which had contracted at the approach of pleasure. I rubbed her slowly. She was there, at my mercy. Rubbing her soon had an effect. She asked me to take off her skirt, which was hanging down over her thighs, and I ran my hand up and down her legs, caressing her. Then I took her buttocks in both hands and rolled them apart. Now it wasn't the ruler which slid between her domes, between the flesh made wet by that burning razor, it was me. I bent over her and gave a few thrusts in order to penetrate her, trying to find the way in by lifting her slightly off the bed. Then I slid my hands on to her breasts, which were crushed by the blouse, and I squeezed them. Then I began to unfasten the blouse and her breasts leapt out, free, into my hands. Her love-making crackled between my fingers as I moved in and out of her rhythmically, sometimes quickly and sometimes slowly. She directed the performance marvellously. And each movement became an explosion of pleasure.

Her body was overcome by a thousand sensations; I was now standing up behind her, and was thrusting the instrument of her pleasure – and my own – into her with all my strength. The lesson continued in a different way.

She went off to fetch a tray. Veronica wanted me to get my strength back after this session. There were cakes and pastries and jam, as well as honey. She wanted to offer herself to me as if she were offering me sweets.

I took the pots of jam and she led me to a low table. She lay down on it and uncovered her breasts. I put some lemon marmalade on the tip of her left breast, then some gooseberry jelly on the right. Those were her orders. Veronica trembled as, little by little, my tongue twisted and turned over the sweet smoothness of her nipples. I must not leave a drop. And I licked her like a starving man, bit into her like a madman. Her globes had swollen under the effect of the waves produced by each paroxysm of sucking, which I repeated at regular intervals. Then she wanted me to take both of them into my mouth at the same time. I pulled them together, pressed them between my fingers and they disappeared into my greedy mouth. She began to melt and I felt a strange substance sticking to a part of me. Veronica had dipped her fingers into the honey-pot and in a flash she had completely covered my prick as well as her cunt. She drew me towards her mouth whilst I moved towards her cunt, which was oozing honey. The sensation was strange and pleasant. Her tongue twisted and darted rapidly, so as not to lose anything. Then I felt her engulfing me in her warm mouth, and she swallowed me completely. She sucked away at me marvellously. She was panting and so was I. Her thighs were twitching involuntarily on either side of my head and we both came together in an explosion of crystallized sugar.

That was the way she learned Spanish with me.

And so, *dear comrade*, those many months in London in Lady Veronica Worthwilde's house were very pleasant – *sweet* even – but I had an idea which would not go away: I must go to Paris. First, I had to convince Lady Veronica that I would be going away.

A few weeks before the date I had set myself, my Venezuelan friend sent me the information I had been waiting for so impatiently.'

'Why did you need this information to go to Paris?' I asked Reinaldo.

'I was sure that this latest news would put me on the trail of my mother. Up till now, my father had always refused to give me any information at all: all I had was a photo. On the back, someone had written "Paris".'

But I asked him if, when he went away, he had left a message for his father. He said not. What fascinated me about him, was this mixture of enthusiasm and gentle melancholy.

'I don't have any regrets,' he said. 'I remember the women I have known. They gave me a lot.'

'Didn't you ever want exclusive rights.'

'No. My life didn't allow me to become attached to just one of them.'

'But when you came to Paris?'

'Things weren't as simple as that,' he said, 'and haven't you yourself ever experienced those dilemmas where reason evaporates in the face of the maddest instincts?'

And Reinaldo continued his story.

'I left London impatiently, but not without memories. When I arrived in Paris, I was armed with a few addresses. I was to go to the house of one of Lady Veronica's old friends, who would provide me with information useful to me in my search. She gave me details relating to organizations spread all over Paris. My task would not be easy, for I had no idea – time was against me – if the people who had known my mother, eighteen years earlier, were still around.

Not far from Gare Saint-Lazare, between rue des Mathurins and rue de Castellane, I settled into little furnished lodgings. I shall always remember that seedy room where I couldn't take one step without falling over the bed or the wash-basin.

But in that area a nocturnal existence was quite exciting for a foreign adolescent who didn't know Paris. I lived amongst prostitutes, artists and a whole cosmopolitan fauna. There was a meeting-place called the Café des Etrangers, on the corner of rue Tronchet and rue de Castellane.

I had chosen this district because it contained a great many nurses and nuns who had served in a military hospital during the war. According to the latest news I had received from my friend, my mother had worked in that hospital.

In my first days in Paris, I went to the consulate,

enrolled on a course to improve my knowledge of French and looked for a job. Then I went sightseeing in the city. I liked walking, and, at night, I walked around place de la Madeleine. For the first time I was approaching the place I was looking for.

One morning, whilst I was drinking a coffee in rue Godot-de-Mauroy, I saw a black woman, dressed in white, sitting opposite me. She was, without a doubt, a nurse. I looked hard at her and caught her gaze. She stared me out, her smile full of naïveté. I had to speak to her. She attracted me, with her big breasts. Just as I was thinking of approaching her, she got up and walked away.

The café owner told me that this woman regularly came here to eat. She was indeed a nurse. I left and went towards Gate Saint-Lazare. It was thronged with people. Early mornings in Paris gave off an atmosphere, a very special ambience, especially in that district. It was all new to me.

Three days later, I met that black woman at the Café des Etrangers again. She was called Nóemie. She was wearing a royal blue hat and a suit which clung to her like a second skin. She was a stylish woman.

At that moment, I told myself that things happen to people if they want them to. I approached her. We had a drink together. I told her a little of my story. Then I told her what I wanted. She had to meet someone, and would be free around ten o'clock. She made fun of my impatience and asked me to meet her in a café near Louis XVI square.

The Café Eden was a pleasant place. At the back, an old piano was playing a popular tune of the day. The tables were separated by booths. Noémie saw me come in and came towards me. She took me towards an empty table, watched with astonishment by her friends, who were standing at the bar.

I then realized that she also lived by her charms. Which explained her complete transformation between early morning and nightfall. First of all, she bought me a drink then introduced me to her friends: Caroline, a very young brunette with curly hair; Juliette, a well-developed blonde; and Béatrice, another brunette, who was older than the others but had one thing they hadn't: class.

Her great dark eyes plunged deep into me; I withstood her devouring gaze, and began to feel at ease with these women. Béatrice called Noémie *Metamorphosis*. And Béatrice answered to the name of *Purgatory*. The four of them formed their own hell, radiating beauty.

One hour later, I followed Noémie home. She lived in a little studio flat in rue d'Isly, only a stone's throw from where I lived. When she took me inside, she switched on a lamp with a blue shade, which cast shadows the colour of Southern seas on to the wallpaper's pattern of little flowers. I felt as though I were rediscovering ancient landscapes . . .

The scent of coriander and cinnamon spread through the room. She stood before me, holding out her arms, and I walked towards her. She murmured

113

words which meant nothing; her quivering lips closed upon mine and her trembling nostrils excited me. We sucked at each other other's lips as though they were some sugary confection. She titillated my ears with her tongue and twisted it around the lobes. I gripped her buttocks, plump as well-rounded gourds. She pushed me over and tore off all my clothes. She stood before me, completely naked, and her jet black flesh was haloed with blue, because of the lighting. Then she drew me towards her body. Her powerful breasts sprang out at me. I took them into my mouth and she made me suck them until her whole body began to tremble. Her nipples, which I nibbled with my teeth, were like firm, elongated cola nuts. I found them infinitely exciting.

Suddenly, she brought her hands back to her breasts, which she squeezed with a sort of pain. She stood up and led me over to the bed, which was covered with a multitude of cushions. She asked me to bite her body all over. I began with her buttocks, then moved upwards along the line of her spinal column. My tongue ran over her neck, under her arms, into her navel – which made her cry out. Her burning flesh contracted at my touch. I was beside myself. She said that she had nothing left to teach me. I doubted that. Then she turned over and began to rub her sap-engorged breasts against my face, my erect prick and the creases of my buttocks. This peculiar moistness intoxicated me unceasingly. This bouquet, which mingled with my sweat, was a powerful aphrodisiac. Our two skins rubbed together like drumsticks on a drum. Nothing could stop us.

Then she took hold of my arms and pulled them apart. She lay on me and rubbed her triangle against my leg, then against my knee. Then she raised herself above me and sucked my lips rapidly and placed her own, like a fiery furnace, upon the erect mask between my legs. As fast as lightning, she twisted her tongue around it. That set me on fire. She drew away and I plunged towards her hips and turned her on to her back. I squeezed her breasts in between my hands, and slid myself into her with little smooth yet jerky movements. Now I was inside her, deep within her.

Pleasure made Noémie laugh. Her body made expressive movements, and I received electric shocks which rose like a fluid from the bottom to the top of my body. Closing her thighs tightly upon me, she told me to hold on firmly and penetrate her very deeply. Then she tightened her massive, fleshy thighs once more around the axis which was working away deep within her flesh. Suddenly, whilst I was continuing to thrust in and out of her, she thrust her pelvis forward, shooting me up into the air. She held on to my buttocks with her hands. I felt as though I were on a switchback railway. I rose and fell, propelled by her. Then her thighs parted. She threw them up into the air again, and repeated the same exercise. She was driving me mad with pleasure. She was in seventh heaven.

Noémie gave me a degree of pleasure which I had

never known before. She was from Guinea, and came originally from Fouta Djalon. She was a woman who only took her pleasure on very rare occasions. She was a prostitute but she had no lover. So I became her lover.

Within a few weeks, I was the privileged friend of all these ladies. By day, they walked the streets, and at night, they worked in the Café Eden. There, I discovered a whole new world. Often, I abandoned my minuscule room to sleep with Noémie, who came home very late. I would wake myself up so as to have a little conversation with her. She would tell me all about her evening, as well as all the gossip concerning their circle of acquaintances.

One day, I was obliged to ask her for help. Béatrice happened to be present, as she was the group's adviser.

You see, I was looking for a job. I had to pay my rent and continue my studies. Of course, they shook their heads. Béatrice looked Noémie straight in the eyes. 'What do you think?' she said. Noémie replied: 'Why not? Let's see.' Béatrice told me that I was lucky to be as handsome as an angel. Then they all burst into sonorous peals of laughter.

'Good, that's settled them,' said Béatrice to me.

'Béatrice and Noémie were my favourites. My new life with them took a surprising turn. Béatrice got me a job as a waiter at the Café Eden. But, what's more, they kept a few extras for me, too.

Béatrice officiated in another pleasure-palace, a well-run house near to Saint-Mandé, at the intersection of Charenton and bois de Vincennes. Three days a week, she hired out her charms in an apartment which had been reserved for her. She had a demanding clientèle but she did not disappoint them.

From the area around rue Madeleine to Gare Saint-Lazare, that was the extent of her territory. She strode up and down the streets, elbowed her way through the crowds, close-packed in places, took her chances and got out of difficult situations.

Thanks to these ladies, I made enormous progress in my knowledge of women. One day, I found a message pushed underneath my door. Noémie wanted me to go round to Béatrice's place.

She lived in rue Duphot, on the top floor of a clean,

middle-class block and she greeted me with a gracious smile. She was wearing a Chinese dressing-gown made of turquoise blue silk. Her hair was combed back, with curls at the sides, and held in place by two golden combs. She affected a cigarette-holder, which she played with like a sensual trumpcard.

The walls of the apartment were papered in mauve. There were many prints of Degas paintings, and a few drawings, portraits of couples. Lamps lit that room dimly, giving a feeling of night.

Once I had sat down, she explained to me the purpose of my visit. She was to initiate me into certain love-games. Games which I should perhaps in future regard as work. Certain women came to the Café Eden to meet young men. Most of them had been abandoned by their husbands, and others came there to add a little spice to their lives. Then there were others – who were taking up the profession of 'enchantress'. They needed advice on the subject.

Through her long years of experience, Béatrice had learned many things about men and women who practise lust. In this way she acquired more and more skills and functions. She began a first, haunting lesson with me.

She lay down on the bed, fully dressed, keeping on her black, high-heeled shoes. And she signalled to me to come and compare her ways with those of Noémie. Her body slid about and stretched like a reptile. When you brushed her skin lightly, electricity spread out from your fingers into the rest of her body. My first meeting with her at the Café Eden had already given me this sensation. A sensation which was about to be reinforced.

She took off my shirt slowly, undoing it button by button, sliding her fingers over my torso in light, sinuous movements. Then, little by little, she nibbled my skin from my neck to my shoulders and then slid down on to my belly. Then she showed me how I was to undress her, in just the right way to expose her to my caresses. But each time she made the exercise trickier, for whilst I was uncovering one part of her body, she was covering up another. She organized her gestures and words like a war strategy. Her orders were implacable. What fascinated me about her was skill in caresses, her slow progressions which amplified pleasure. Her hands flew towards me, in precise lines, making me shiver all over. Her fine, soft lips closed like carnivorous plants on their prey. I felt the bud open and I was borne away as though by a typhoon. Slowly at first, then more and more quickly, and once again slowly at the finish.

Now on my belly, I was under her sway. She went up and down my body, rubbing me with the hard, wrinkled tips of her fruits. Suddenly her tongue became viperine, flashing through the furrow between the valleys. The heat became more and more intense. Her breathing quickened. I was all aglow. We were now on the edge of the bed. She put one leg on the ground and left the other on the bed. I slid around her and took her in the slender gap offered by her body. My hands clung to her breasts. Then, twisting round, I pushed my head forward to suck one of them. As she arched her body and I contorted mine, we brought together prick and cunt.

Welded to me, Béatrice trembled, consuming me with pleasures. Hers was an awesome lesson.

When I took up my post at the Café Eden, I felt full of confidence. Noémie came looking for me, to get the latest news. I told her that everything had gone well.

One day, Noémie took me back home with her. She told me that everyone in the place where she worked during the day had known my mother very well. During the war, she had served in various hospices, alongside the nuns. It was also known that she had married a foreigner, a South American, and that she left with him to go back there. One of these nurses had changed her job and had met up with my mother two years later, once again in Paris. They had been friends and had later changed over to restaurant work. My mother worked in the best places in Paris.

Noémie showed me three large restaurants where she had been seen. Perhaps I might be able to meet people who had known her. But it was a strong possibility that, under her real name or under her maiden name, I would have some difficulty in finding her.

I thought of the photo which never left me. I told Noémie about it. She wanted to see her face. She was none the wiser. This photo was old, that would not make my search any easier. At the earliest opportunity, she would take this photo to her hospital and show it to the oldest nurses.

I reported to the cashier; she called a middle-aged man and had a conversation with him.

When he came towards me, he began to recall a woman who used to work there many years ago. He remembered that she had been married in South America. She had a French name when she came to work in this restaurant. He went off to find an address book and checked to see if he had noted down her exact name and address. Alas . . . He asked me to come back in case he found the addresses of friends who might be able to give me information.

I continued my search, and went into two other large Paris cafés. Still nothing. I returned to the first café-restaurant. My old gentleman hadn't uncovered any trails. I showed him the photo, and he recognized it but she was called 'Lise' and not 'Louise', as I had told him.

I thought that I would never pick up my mother's trail.

The Café Eden sparkled with a thousand bright lights. Girls arrived from the four corners of France, some prettier than others. Béatrice, who was the queen and mistress of the whole place, retired. Noémie replaced her and organized everything with Caroline.

I was becoming an adult without realizing it. I began to play a more and more important role in the evenings organized by Noémie and Caroline. The

121

pleasure of the flesh became a part of my life. So you see, *dear companion*, I became a sort of libertine who didn't refuse any experience, any adventure. What adolescent could have lived what I have lived? How many caresses did I receive, and how many have I given?

And yet, even now, my feelings are still as intense and as fresh as they always were.'

I asked Reinaldo if he had continued to live like that for long.

'For a while.'

'Beatrice, the *femme fatale*, introduced me to a house at Saint-Mandé, not far from Charenton and bois de Vincennes. The surroundings provided a complete change from the centre of Paris. Here, there was greenery and calm. That great secluded house, nestling deep in large, verdant gardens, belonged to a lady whose identity I did not know. I left the Café Eden. Noémie followed Béatrice to this new place. They needed a receptionist, and I took on the job. I had a few other tasks, too. But mostly I had to screen and control the rowdy arrivals of certain half-drunken men. Béatrice acted as mistress of the establishment, presenting the girls and praising their *qualities*.

When Béatrice was busy, an old gentleman officiated at the entrance. We immediately got to know each other and became good friends.

He had succeeded in setting up his house with a few friends and girls ready to follow him, and he had worked very hard.

I then told him about my journey from La Guaira to Paris. I was an adventurer, just as much as he was, he told me. But when I was with him I never referred to the real goal of my journey. What's more, I had given up dreaming about my mother.

When I wasn't working, my free time was devoted to study. And I continued to visit Paris, which I loved passionately.

In time, I came to know all the girls in the house. Listen to me once more, *dear comrade*.

One of them was of Spanish origin. She was twenty-two. And she had lived in this house for three years. She had earned the nickname of *The Madonna*, as she was always raising her eyes to Heaven. That did not prevent her being seductive or having a sense of humour. The young *Madonna* only appeared towards the end of the afternoon. She was on duty at night.

In that house, the things which had intrigued me most were the signs on the doors of the bedrooms where the girls received their clients. They all alluded to works of literature.

I had to intervene on several occasions, on certain nights, when clients were too exuberant and alcohol-sodden, and threatened to cause trouble, and even – who knows – a drama. . . .'

I wanted Reinaldo to tell me about those famous nights. And so he continued:

'The first night began with the following scene: *The She-Wolf of the Steppes*. It was the incarnation of the sixth sin: *Anger*. Sonia, a blonde with bouffant hair, and blue eyes which attracted you to her magnetically, and an abundant figure, gave free rein to her sexual instincts, which were not without their aggressive side. You were the beneficiary. And so it happened that I was present at this famous scene. She covered herself with a cape made from remnants of fur. Then she slid on to the ground, were there lay a child's sledge and reins. She crawled over to me and held out the reins to me, smiling. I realized that she was inviting me to play with her. She asked me to sit astride her and made me do a circuit of the bedroom. Then she laid me down, completely naked, on the sledge and tied me up with the reins. She threw her cape over me. I then felt her lowering herself in between my legs. She ran her tongue over my thighs whilst positioning her hands around my hips. Her hands moved upwards vigorously, then let go, leaving me in a state of painful expectancy. She then reversed her movements, which were full of unbridled sensuality. Then she rubbed her heavy breasts against my face: and I moved my mouth, trying to bite them. Her vulva came towards my lips and brushed against them. She was above me and constantly moving up and down my imprisoned body. Suddenly she sat down on my

125

prick, which she had been licking. When my horn was deep within her, she moved backwards and forwards as though she were astride a mount. Her thrusts made me rock to and fro on the sledge, which was very pleasant. The counterbalance accentuated the pleasure all the more. Eventually, I was rocking with pleasure. The more I displayed it, the more she speeded up her up-and-down movements. When her pleasure was upon her, she began a song which mingled with my cries of pleasures. And her body, above mine, beat the rhythm more and more frantically. She described the vibrations which were mounting within her. I exploded and asked her to untie me. She left.

I hurriedly brought myself to my senses and went about my duties.

For me, time could no longer be measured precisely.

One evening, when I arrived at the house, I was rather surprised to find all the girls in a state of excitement. Béatrice announced that she had found a room for me. So I could leave my bedsit. Madame Lisa had a spare room in an apartment which adjoined the house of pleasure. She was putting it at my disposal in recognition of my good service.

I was pleased with my new space. Béatrice had arranged things nicely. So I invited Noémie and Béatrice to a champagne celebration that very evening.

After that interlude, I felt a desire to spend my night

with the girl who embodied *Gluttony*, the fifth sin, and who was known as *Little Red Riding Hood*. That was the name given to Sophie, whose body looked like that of a little girl with all her innocence peeled away – a fact which made her extremely desirable. Sophie wore red dresses with flounces, in the Spanish fashion. She was a brunette with hair tumbling down her back, and on her feet she wore light ballet-shoes. You couldn't help noticing her because she was always playing with ribbons which she would take out of her pockets at any moment. She was lightly made-up.

I followed her into her room, noticing that she owned a selection of the sort of outfits worn by model little girls, like the ones Lewis Carroll loved. She began by playing hard to get. She cowered in the corner, whining and wriggling about. So I pretended to lose my patience. 'You're not going to smack my bottom,' she told me. I walked towards her and dragged her away, lifting her up. I sat down on a chair, held her to me and tore off her lace panties. I bounced her up and down on my knee whilst I undid my flies. 'Give me a smacked bottom,' she continued. Lifting up her skirts, I gave her backside a preliminary slap. She stood up and bent over on a level with the opening in my trousers. I continued to spank her until the moment when I felt she was getting wet. Now she spread her legs and moved her head with a circular motion. She stuck out her tongue whilst I felt myself getting harder and harder. Then I allowed her to have a well-deserved lollipop. First, her greedy mouth swallowed me to the hilt. She took my hand and guided it between her buttocks. I began to masturbate her to the rhythm of her greedy sucking. Her acrobatics and her balance excited me more and more. She moved from left to right, keeping the lollipop in her mouth.

When the lollipop melted in her mouth, she began to wheedle and coax. So I took her in my arms and fondled her as she asked me to.

The other girls saw me coming out of the room of special delights, and rushed to tell me to make myself scarce, as important people were waiting at reception to have their turn with greedy Red Riding Hood.

My sense of time was becoming flawed and indistinct.

I continued my experiments, paying a visit to the *Dairymaid with the Milk-jug* – that was Geneviève. On her door there was an engraving of a country scene, representing *Sloth*, or the seventh sin. Looking at her powerful chest, it seemed that it contained a secret activity, hidden underneath her clothes. It was a independent organ, overflowing with life. When one of her breasts thrust forward under this formidable pressure of sensuality, I knew that it must be put back in place quickly. That was the ritual. Next, they both popped out together, and I squeezed them whilst she encircled my hips with her arms. Then she gave them to me to suckle. Each of them took its turn in my mouth. Her nipples were rounded like cherries. I had to roll them between my teeth. After that, she wedged my head in the hollow of her breasts, and I could hear her heart beating.

Having got past the wet-nurse stage, she organized a second game. She spread a runny cream all over her breasts. Then she told me to turn round. At her signal, I discovered that she had arranged a skirt under her bosom, turning them into two hillocks that looked just like a well-formed backside. She invited me to insert my prick between her two creamy globes. I took up my position on her belly, and – with my hands on either side of her body – I slid into that little valley. I thrust in and out; she followed me, harmonizing with my rhythm. My prick had swollen more than usual. Next, she made me lie down on my back whilst she skimmed the surface of my belly and my rock-hard prick with her breasts. This went on until at last I burst forth.

Next, you could go and see Karine, the girl from Alsace, who was known as the *Venus in Furs*. Her desires were impure. Throngs of men came to see her. Her nickname was *Lust*, and you couldn't but agree with it. To have had both of them in the same evening would have killed me.

But I did have an opportunity to be present at one of her sessions. Karine strode into the drawing-room, a fur coat slung over her shoulders. Her hips swayed, and a long dress clung tightly to her figure. Her body rippled, like a siren's. Her laced-up ankle-boots accentuated her lascivious look. Those who desired her were fascinated by her boots, her laces. She took a whip out of the cupboard and made her 'guest' run about, threatening him with that whip. Then she would tame him as she would have tamed a dog, bringing him to heel and showing off his tricks.

I had a weakness for Brigitte, *The Confessor*. She was a strange mixture: she had a taste for happiness, but also for the unhappiness of others. She was *Envy*. With her, you were allowed to talk; she would let you pour out your heart in interminable confessions. She understood our desires. If I should wish to lie down in the darkness, she was eager to put me at my ease; if I wanted slow caresses or massages, she would give them to me. One evening, when I had no desire for physical communion, I allowed her to lick my cock and it grew little by little, in jerky movements. She took me into her mouth and swallowed me down gradually, then drew back and nibbled me gently. The apotheosis was when she bore down on me and engulfed me in the hollow of her backside. She rose and fell with her usual slowness. She clenched her muscles and her agility sent a thousand sensations running through my body.

She was a sort of regenerative sauna of sexuality. That was what she had in common with *The Orient Express*, the nickname given to the enigmatic and voluptuous Anita. She was of mixed parentage: a pinch of the Orient and a pinch of Asia. She sported a long ivory cigarette-holder, inlaid with rings of ebony. She was always gazing at something far away and inaccessible. From time to time, she would stare at you for a long time, then smile and wink at you. She ran her tongue over her lips, lasciviously. She inflamed your senses by crossing and uncrossing her legs. With great subtlety, she gave herself not as others gave themselves, but through a series of entirely perverse surrenders. *Avarice* suited her to a T. Her room was done out like a *wagon-lit*. According to her ritual, she slowly undid my flies and knotted her dress around her hips. Then she made a pirouette: she lifted one leg as high as she could and slid it along the wall, at the height of my shoulders. I pointed myself towards her cunt. But I now had some difficulty in entering her, as she was hopping about. The game excited me more and more. Her breasts pushed closed against my chest. I felt the nipples. I spread her legs. And, balancing her, I lifted her and quickly pushed in my prick. But I had to thrust it in firmly and hold on to keep it in there. Suddenly she asked me to hold on tight to her hips; she pressed herself even harder against me and lifted her other leg. Now she was more or less doing the splits against the wall. So I was able to thrust deep into her. She was exceptionally ingenious and she knew it only too well. The great depth of her cunt allowed me to be completely in between her thighs whilst I tried to cling on to her small, rounded buttocks. I thrust in and out whilst she kept on thrusting into the air, against the walls. At the end, she brought her legs down again and slid them along mine, squeezing my imprisoned prick very hard. Once again she hopped up and down and I felt the urge to ejaculate. I felt everything growling and rumbling. And in a flash she released her embrace. She swayed backwards a little and once again placed her leg on my shoulder. And once again I lifted her up. So I was able to take her deep down, putting her other leg on my other shoulder. Her litheness astonished me once again. She put one leg on the ground, then the other. She turned round so that her back was towards me. She guided my prick into her and held it there firmly with her hand. I was completely dumbfounded, as I was still erect and this last operation ended in an eruption of burning lava. I completely soaked her whilst she squeezed her buttocks against my prick. I then pulled her two globes apart and rubbed my prick along her little fluted corolla. With a thrust of her backside, she made me enter her again. I was immediately in the depths of a volcano and I gave a long cry of ecstasy. At that moment, she began to moan louder and louder, and hopped up and down once more before abandoning herself entirely to her orgasm.

Anita's fiery temperament consumed us in our entirety.

Whenever I became melancholy, Beatrice would tell me to go and see the *Fisher of Souls*, Marguerite. Everything in her conjured up *Pride*. Her secret was the spoken word. She enchanted you with her vocabulary, which was full of images; the precision of her words; and the tone of her voice. When you clung on to her as you would cling to a life-buoy, she became a mother, then your first love, and finally your divine mistress. She made you progress from childhood to adulthood with appropriate games. For some of us, Marguerite was a bouquet of flowers.

When men wanted to indulge in the *Seven Deadly Sins*, they always went to Marguerite.

I remember all of these women, *dear comrade*, because they taught me a great deal.

At last, I caught sight of the lady who ran this great dwelling. More than a month had gone by before I saw her.

I shall always remember that afternoon. I had gone for a walk near the little lake at Saint-Mandé.

I was in the drawing-room. A door opened and closed on an apparition: an elegant woman with lithe, graceful bearing. She was wearing dark glasses. This was Madame Lisa, the mistress of the establishment. The image of this woman became fixed in my memory. And each time I recalled it, I experienced a strange sensation – one which I had experienced before.

One afternoon, whilst crossing the corridor which led to my room, I saw a shaft of light. I realized that the door to Madame Lisa's apartment was open. Curiosity got the better of me. I approached the open doorway, walking very softly. I felt attracted; I pushed the door open as if someone was waiting for me. I went in. The apartment was limited to one very large, octagonal room, divided into separate areas by screens and hangings. I spotted a bed flanked by two chests-of-drawers, and not far away a desk on which I could make out two photos. That's when I was overcome with amazement.

The only sound was the muffled thumping of my heart as I looked closely at a *portrait* framed in the old-fashioned way. On the desk sat the shot which had followed me for so many years.

I was dumbfounded.

In another snapshot, I recognized my father. And *Her*, by his side – was that my mother?

I picked up the photo to check that I was right.

Memories rose up within me. Something told me that my journey was now ending.

For several days, I abandoned the house and the girls. I didn't want to see or hear anything. When Béatrice and Noémie met me by chance in the street, I told them everything. I hadn't yet got quite to the heart of the matter.

I was waiting for a sign, a sign from *Her*.

Six days later, I learned that a change had taken place in this woman's life. Béatrice told me that her behaviour had changed since I had gone into her apartment. She was no longer seen in public. The girls said that she was ill.

At last, I saw *Her*.

She wasn't wearing the glasses any more. I found it difficult to look into her eyes. She said to me, very gently:

'Hello . . . young man.'

Rooted to the spot, I blurted out a few inaudible words. I can still remember the scent of her body, the way her voice trembled, her gestures.

From that day on, my life was changed.'

Reinaldo agreed to give me the last key to his story. So the reunion had taken place. *She*, the *Lady* for that was what they called her, was his mother. But in spite of his explanations I didn't understand if she had been a nurse or a former nun. For him, that was the same thing, or almost. When she met his father, they had married and left together for Venezuela. They lived together for about a year and a half. Then she left him to return to France. She had been unable to adapt to that country, to relations with a husband, a husband who was very often not there. As for his father, Reinaldo learned of his death about fifteen years ago, during an industrial expedition into the Colombian forest, in the early Seventies. This loss had strengthened the ties with his mother.

He had shown a degree of discomfort at the end of the story about his mother. He had sensed that I was perhaps waiting for something else.

Indeed, I knew a part of his love life. But would

Reinaldo tell me what happened to his mother? Had she been in close contact since their reunion?

'I don't know, *dear comrade*, if you have quite understood the vicissitudes of my life. It was sometimes difficult for me to see them clearly myself. I rushed headlong into life, and it absorbed me. Sometimes I found it excessively beautiful, sometimes excessively bitter. Pleasures have been my consolation. And today, I have realized my original goal.'

Reinaldo added nonchalantly:

'It was you yourself who prompted me to speak. Without this conversation, I would not have understood certain elements of my adolescent life. But all that is only a part of my life!'

He surprised me yet again.

We remained in silence for a moment, both of us picking up our glasses for a toast.

'Last orders, please!' announced the bartender.

The bar was now completely empty.

On the juke-box, Nina Simone was singing *My Way*.

Dawn was breaking.

Just as we were about to leave, the door opened a little way. . . .

'Reinaldo, it's time: come on,' called a woman dressed all in black. I could only just see her standing there. He wished me goodnight and went off to join her.

I saw them walking away from me, arm in arm, across the Carrefour de l'Odéon.

His step was confident and serene. But who was the woman he was walking with?